# Spooky Stories from the Swamp

# Spooky Stories from the Swamp

## Tales from the Florida Back Country

Doug Alderson

PINEAPPLE PRESS
*Palm Beach, Florida*

Unless otherwise indicated, all photos are by the author.

Pineapple Press
An imprint of The Rowman & Littlefield Publishing Group, Inc.
4501 Forbes Blvd., Ste. 200
Lanham, MD 20706
www.rowman.com

Distributed by NATIONAL BOOK NETWORK

British Library Cataloguing in Publication Information available

**Library of Congress Cataloging-in-Publication Data available**

Names: Alderson, Doug, author.
Title: Spooky stories from the swamp : tales from the Florida back country / Doug
    Alderson.
Description: Lanham : Pineapple Press, 2020. | Summary: "Florida's famous swamps-
    from the Everglades to Mosquito Lagoon to Tate's Hell-serve as fitting backdrops for
    these chilling original stories. Maybe it's because they are often wet, shadowy places of
    wild beauty where few people dare to penetrate. They are havens for snakes, alligators,
    black bears, wildcats, and who knows what. People on the run have often hidden in
    swamps, while others have gotten lost in the watery expanses; the swamp can be a
    refuge or a nightmare. Mysterious things just happen in swamps. Maybe it's because
    they are often wet, shadowy places of wild beauty where few people dare to penetrate.
    They are havens for snakes, alligators, black bears, wildcats, and who knows what.
    People on the run have often hidden in swamps, while others have gotten lost in the
    watery expanses; the swamp can be a refuge or a nightmare. Where else can you find
    a ghost baby, or an angry specter, or a lost soul? How about a   ghost who is obsessed
    with the ghost orchid, or an alluring snake woman? Throw in a skunk ape or two and
    you've got the ingredients for many entertaining hours sharing these stories around a
    campfire or reading them to yourself or out loud"—Provided by publisher.
Identifiers: LCCN 2019052785 (print) | LCCN 2019052786 (ebook) | ISBN
    9781683340843 (paperback) | ISBN 9781683340850 (epub)
Subjects: LCSH: Tales—Florida. | Legends—Florida. | Swamps—Florida—Folklore.
Classification: LCC GR110.F5 A5324 2020  (print) | LCC GR110.F5  (ebook) | DDC
    398.209759—dc23
LC record available at https://lccn.loc.gov/2019052785
LC ebook record available at https://lccn.loc.gov/2019052786

For Cheyenne.
May you always be in touch with your inner child.

# Contents

# Foreword

Storytelling is an endangered art form, threatened by computers, video games, television, and movies. When I started leading camping trips with groups of young people, good old-fashioned storytelling became my salvation. A spellbinding tale of mystery and intrigue could keep my group entertained and focused, easing pangs of withdrawal from modern electronic distractions, and sometimes reducing the likelihood of someone wandering off in the dark. My sanity, and those of fellow counselors, was better ensured, and the stories sometimes had an impact.

Returning campers often remembered certain stories and chimed in if I left out a part. Inevitably, some would ask, "Is that really true?" I learned from other storytellers to always reply with a "Yes," or "What do you think?" thereby increasing their sense of wonder. After all, most good stories have elements of truth in them where the line between fact and fiction is difficult to distinguish.

Many of these stories have environmental, historical, and cultural themes. While entertaining, they can also teach. Florida is rich in history, natural beauty, and ecological and cultural diversity. In order to protect what is special about our state, we must educate the people who live here and those who are coming to live or visit. Textbooks can be dry and are not always the best tools for teaching and learning. Tales of mystery and intrigue, interwoven with important facts and lessons, just might be the ticket.

# Acknowledgments

*I* would like to acknowledge several adult counselors with whom I shared many a journey and whose stories I admire. Claude Stephens, Jim Lollis, and John Schaller are among this group. Several outstanding students stand out in my mind, but unfortunately, I've forgotten the names of some. Most are now adults with children, and I hope they are weaving tales of their own. A few I want to mention are Paul Ingram, Holly Loveland, Jamie Lollis, and Rodney Felix.

I want to thank the Tallahassee Museum for giving me the opportunity to hone my craft. I trust that the museum's educational programs and summer camps will continue to spawn future storytellers and raise awareness about Florida's history, environment, and diverse cultures.

# Introduction

$\mathscr{M}$ysterious things happen in swamps. Maybe it's because they are often wet, shadowy places of wild beauty where few people dare to penetrate. They are havens for snakes, alligators, black bears, wildcats, and who knows what else.

People on the run have often hid in swamps, while others have gotten lost in the watery expanses; the swamp could be a refuge or a nightmare.

In *Spooky Stories from the Swamp*, there's a bit of everything, such as how people have viewed swamps for example. You'll also learn how Florida's famous swamps—from the Everglades to Mosquito Lagoon to Tate's Hell— serve as fitting backdrops for these chilling original stories. Where else but a swamp can you find a ghost baby, an angry specter, or a lost soul? How about a ghost who is obsessed with the rare ghost orchid or an alluring snake woman? Throw in a skunk ape or two and you've got the ingredients for many entertaining hours of sharing stories around a campfire or reading them to yourself or out loud. And from the author's notes at the end of each story, you might learn a thing or two about Florida's swamps, creatures, and history as well as storytelling tips. So, turn the page if you dare!

# Ghost Baby

*S*igns marking the town where I grew up listed its founding as 1851, but everyone in my neighborhood knew of a graveyard down the old swamp road that was older than that. Weathered gravestones listed death dates in the 1830s. No one knew where these early people had come from, or why they lived on a small island in a cypress swamp when there was plenty of dry land elsewhere.

Mrs. Johnson, my neighbor, claimed they had been gypsies running from the law. That's what she had heard growing up, and she was more than eighty years old. But Mr. Tucker at the fire station swore they had been witches— they lived in the swamp so no one would bother them, and they made potions with water moccasin venom. We weren't sure if that was just a story told to scare us, or if it was true.

Sometimes we'd hear strange noises coming from the swamp, mostly on calm evenings just past sunset. This was the twilight time folks called dark-thirty because that's when the spirits roamed. Some said the sound was from a moaning ghost; others thought it was more like crying, a child's or a baby's cry. My parents said it was just the wind, a screech owl, or maybe a lonesome dog. It did sound lonely, but it didn't sound like any dog I had ever heard. It made me feel cold inside, even on a warm summer's night.

Loggers built the road that led through the swamp in the early 1900s. They raised it above the water by digging ditches on both sides. They put a rail line on top and hauled out the heavy cypress logs with a steam locomotive. They cut big pines off the island, too, but they left the old graveyard alone, a place where cedar and pine trees stood tall. Mrs. Johnson said the loggers refused to camp on the island because they heard eerie sounds coming from the graveyard, especially at dark-thirty. It was haunted, they said. That's why they left the trees.

When the loggers finished their work, they took out the rail lines and left the high railbed to be used as a road. The old swamp road was never paved, and it became thick with soft sand during dry periods. We'd sometimes ride our bikes down it, especially in summer because it was a shortcut to the city park, but we'd only go during daytime. No one lived in the swamp, so there were no streetlights. Plus, riding by the old graveyard was spooky, even in bright sunlight. We'd sometimes do it on a dare.

One summer afternoon my brother Dave and I rode our bikes to the city park to swim and play games. We became caught up in a ping-pong tournament in the park's indoor recreation center and by the time we stepped outside, we took one look at the sunset sky and began to panic. "We'll have to ride back by the swamp road," said Dave.

"No way," I protested. "No one goes that way this time of day."

"It's that or be grounded. We add twenty minutes going the other way." Dave spoke without a hint of fear in his voice. I glared at him, but I knew he was right. We had only two weeks remaining of our summer vacation and we didn't want to spend it restricted to our house and yard. We set off riding as fast as we could.

By the time we reached the swamp road, the western sky was a brilliant orange. Some other time we would have stopped to enjoy the sunset, but

**Headstones from the 1800s, like the ones described in "Ghost Baby."**

we knew we had to get home as soon as possible. It hadn't rained in almost a month; however the road was so soft that no matter how hard we tried to pedal, we had to walk our bikes past the old graveyard. That's when we heard the noise.

"What's that?" Dave asked, stopping.

"I don't know, and I don't care," I replied, feeling a sense of panic. I tried to run in the soft sand but couldn't go very fast. It reminded me of certain dreams—something was chasing me, but I couldn't run fast enough to get away.

Dave followed, but he abruptly stopped again. "Listen!" he said. "It sounds like someone crying. Like, a baby crying." We had a younger brother, so we were familiar with crying babies, but this was different, more desperate.

"It's probably just a screech owl," I said. "Let's go!"

"Maybe someone left him," said Dave. He didn't move. We had heard stories of people leaving babies at churches and on people's doorsteps, but never in a graveyard. Dave, being older, put down his bike and announced, "We've got to find out."

"No," I said, "it's spooky."

"We have to," said Dave. "The baby may need our help."

I took a deep breath. That graveyard was the last place I wanted to walk into, especially at dark-thirty, but I reluctantly agreed.

As we pushed our way through brambles and vines, past live oak, cedar, and pine, the crying grew louder. Finally we rounded a tree and saw it—a small baby wrapped in an old blanket laying in a shallow depression. He cried louder when he saw us.

"What do we do now?" I asked, petrified.

"Well," said Dave, "we've got to take him home with us."

"No way. Are you crazy? What will Mom and Dad say when we show up with a baby?"

"We can't just leave him here," said Dave.

I exhaled loudly. We had to decide quickly because it was getting dark. "Oh, I guess you're right," I said. Dave was usually right, but I rarely admitted it out loud. This occasion was an exception.

Dave gently reached down and picked up the baby. Immediately, it stopped crying and started doing a kind of cooing sound. Dave managed to smile. "He's kind of cute," he said, "and he's light as a feather, or maybe he is a she." He checked and announced, "It's a he." He gave him to me to hold. Surprisingly, the baby was much lighter than our younger brother, although they appeared to be the same age—maybe four or five months old.

"I wonder how long he's been out here," I said nervously, looking around. It wasn't a place where I would want to hang out. Deep shadows stretched beneath moss-draped branches. Tree frogs and cicadas called in rhythmic choruses, creating a strange pulsing sound, like a loud heartbeat. Mosquitoes buzzed in my ear.

"We'd better go," said Dave.

We started toward the road. Maybe I was more tired than I thought, but the baby seemed to be getting heavier with each step. "Hey Dave, you carry him," I said. "My arms are hurting."

Dave smirked. "We haven't even gone fifty feet." He reluctantly took the baby. He only made it another twenty feet before he started complaining. "Gee, you're right. This baby is getting heavy."

In another minute, we both had to carry the baby; Dave cradled the head and upper back while I held his butt and legs. The baby now weighed more than our German shepherd at home. This was getting weird. I glanced down at the baby and nearly dropped him in the road. "DDDave," I stuttered. "Lll-looooook."

Dave looked down and nearly dropped his end of the baby. Smiling up at us was no longer the face of a baby but that of an old man, gray-haired and wrinkled. "What do we do now?" I whispered, stiff with fear.

"We have to take him back," Dave whispered. Dave always seemed to have an answer for everything. I admired him for that, and was a little envious, but Dave didn't always give good reasons for his answers and this was one of those times.

"How come?" I asked.

"How come what?"

"How come we have to take him back?" My voice shook. I didn't want to return to that spooky graveyard.

Dave's voice lowered even more to where I could barely hear him. "I think he's a ghost baby," he said. "If we leave him in the road, there's no telling what might happen."

I'm not sure what made Dave the ghost expert at that moment, but strangely, his answer made sense. We reluctantly turned around and headed back toward the graveyard. As we did, the baby became lighter and the old man's face gradually returned to that of a baby. Near dark, when we finally laid the ghost baby back down on what must have been the shallow depression of his grave, he started crying again. "What do we do now?" I asked, panicked. I felt like crying too.

For the first time, a frightened look came across Dave's face. "Let's get the hell out of here!" he said.

He didn't need to say it twice. We ran out of that graveyard, tripping over headstones and falling into brush. When we reached the sandy road, we ran right past our bikes and kept going.

Arriving home breathless and well past dark, we burst through the door and gave Mom and Dad the whole story in about fifteen seconds. It went something like this: "Mom, Dad, we're sorry we're late, but we were riding back by the old graveyard and we heard a baby crying, so we checked it out and found a baby! But when we started carrying it home, it wasn't a baby, it turned into an old man, so we had to take it back to its grave or it would haunt us forever. Then we ran as fast as we could all the way back home. So that's why we were late!"

It wasn't fun to be grounded for the last two weeks of summer vacation, but we now knew the source of the lonely cry that crept through the night air like swamp fog.

## AUTHOR'S NOTES

"Ghost Baby" was inspired from reading a brief description of a similar story in *Ghost Stories from the American South*, a scholarly work compiled and edited by W. K. McNeil. I was collecting spooky stories to share at an upcoming Halloween gathering and was searching for last minute inspiration. I wrapped a personal story around this old tale, stretching a two-paragraph story into one that lasted about fifteen minutes. The audience was spellbound and "Ghost Baby" turned into a personal favorite.

According to McNeil's research, ghost baby stories are often associated with Mexicans and Mexican Americans, and with people from other Latin American countries. These stories can involve the baby growing a gray beard, or sharp teeth or fangs. Sometimes the baby grows larger, not just heavier, and turns into a type of devil, with claws, horns, and tail. Some versions have the "baby" dropped and it disappears, or it must be returned to the graveyard, as was the case in the story I shared.

## MORE ABOUT SWAMPS, LOGGING, AND GRAVEYARDS

Florida's cypress trees were once reminiscent of the California redwoods due to their size. Massive cypresses, sometimes thousands of years old, reached lofty heights up to 150 feet, with buttressed bases of 30 feet or more in circumference. In prelogging days, giant cypress trees dominated many of Florida's forested swamps, casting a thick veil of shade in the growing season. Smaller trees and dormant seeds seemingly waited in anticipation for one of the larger trees to fall from a storm, lightning, or old age. Then, they hastened to flourish in the new window of light.

A hiker stands next to an old cypress tree that may be centuries old.

The largest old-growth bald cypress forest that remains in North America is the National Audubon Society's thirteen-thousand-acre Corkscrew Swamp Sanctuary near Naples. Visitors can also see old-growth bald cypress along the Tamiami Trail in the Fakahatchee Strand State Preserve.

Logging of Florida's cypress forests began in earnest in the early 1900s and continued through the 1940s. Logging cypress trees first involved girdling them by notching around their base so the sap would run down, starving the trunk. The final cutting would not occur for several months. In the meantime, loggers often built a grid of raised railbeds or trams so logs could be moved out of the forest. In the early days, men worked six- to nine-foot crosscut saws. The toppled trees were trimmed and then hooked to long cables connected to a steam-powered rotating drum known as a power skidder, which sat on a rail line. Once the power skidder began pulling an enormous tree, everything in its path was crushed as the log plowed through the swamp's soft bottom. Logging accidents were common. Once dragged parallel to the tracks, the cypress logs were loaded onto railcars with cranes and taken to a sawmill.

A logger's day often began with a wake-up call or whistle at 4:30 a.m. Breakfast usually consisted of fried fat pork, biscuits, syrup, and coffee. Around

6:00 a.m., a train carried the loggers to the work area, and then back to camp after ten or twelve hours of hard work.

Today, cypresses are still logged for their wood, but young trees are often cut for landscaping mulch. It is feared that cypress trees in Florida are being cut at a rate faster than they can naturally grow or regrow. Conservationists are urging consumers to purchase pine bark or melaleuca mulch (made from an invasive exotic species) to reduce the pressure on cypress forests.

While early graveyards were not normally established in cypress swamps, they were established on adjacent lands and on pine islands, such as the one depicted in "Ghost Baby." If gravestones were visible or the graveyard known, loggers often respected these graveyards and did not harvest the trees, thus the reason why graveyards often harbor the largest trees in an area. In the Midwest, some of the last native prairie plants can be found in graveyards and along railbeds.

## STORYTELLING TIPS

"Ghost Baby" is best told in dim light with enough room to move around. Try to imitate a crying baby, one that is desperate sounding. Done properly, this will send a chill through your audience. You don't need to move around much until you enter the graveyard. Then you can pretend to be pushing your way through brush and stepping over headstones. When you reach the "baby," bend over, soften your voice, and carefully lift with outstretched arms. Your listeners will easily visualize it, making it even more shocking when you begin straining your arms from the steadily increasing weight, and the "baby" turns into an old man.

Speed up your dialogue at the end to convey a sense of panic.

**Estimated Telling Time:** 11–12 minutes

# • 2 •

# The Ghost Orchid Ghost

Fakahatchee Strand is one of Florida's most beautiful swamps. The first thing that strikes visitors are the royal palms. They tower over the cypress, maple, and pop ash trees, giving the swamp a tropical look. Then there are the ferns. Sword ferns can be as tall as a man and cover the forest floor. Walking and wading through this jungle, a person can feel small, very small.

Several endangered Florida panthers call Fakahatchee home, too, but the great swamp is probably best known for its intricate wild orchids, especially the rare ghost orchid. In order to see the ghost orchid, you have to earn it. It doesn't grow along the roadside; it grows in the wet part of the swamp. And it doesn't bloom in winter when it is cool and biting insects are more tolerable. The ghost orchid blooms in summer, the hottest part of the year and a time when mass numbers of mosquitoes feed with fervor.

Despite these difficulties, orchid enthusiasts arrive from all over the world to glimpse Fakahatchee's famous ghost orchid, and a few come to steal it. For certain people, collecting orchids is more than a hobby—it is an obsession. The indescribable attraction and intoxicating aromas of select orchids have driven collectors mad with greed. The craze peaked in the late 1800s when collectors from England and other countries traveled the world in search of rare specimens, sometimes enduring rugged conditions and hostile people. Millions of orchids were stripped from their native forests.

One August day I sought to find a blooming ghost orchid in Fakahatchee. A ranger described a general area to search after I convinced him I only wanted to photograph it. I support the law against collecting wild orchids. If too many people take something this rare from nature, the species will become extinct in the wild. Then the ghost orchid will indeed become a ghost.

The thick growth found in Fakahatchee Strand State Preserve.

**Swamp opening in Fakahatchee Strand State Preserve.**

I questioned my sanity as I began wading into waist-deep dark water, not knowing if I was stepping on a log or an alligator. I spotted a couple of snakes, though luckily no water moccasins. Mosquitoes pestered me constantly, and in one of the few dry spots amid a clump of orange mushrooms, I found the unmistakable track of a Florida panther. Normally, a panther track would excite me, but on this day, alone in Fakahatchee with the lush growth obscuring my view, it was a little spooky. I felt vulnerable, even though I knew panthers have not been known to attack people since the pioneer days of the 1800s. But it wasn't a panther cry that caused me to jump. It was a moan, a very human moan. Someone was in distress!

Cautiously, I moved forward and was surprised to find a man dressed in loose beige khakis and wearing a type of safari pith helmet, like what I had seen worn by European adventurers in old photographs. "Why?" he kept repeating. "Why?" He was standing in knee-deep water, leaning against a cypress trunk. His accent was either English or Australian.

"Can I help you?" I interrupted.

The man froze and looked up. His eyes were bloodshot, like he had been crying, and he was pale as a ghost. "No one can help me," he said. "I am cursed."

"Cursed?" I asked, confused.

"Yes, cursed," he said. "Look at it. It is so beautiful. So, so beautiful."

He nodded toward a ghost orchid in full bloom, its pencil-thick stem wrapped around a small tree trunk. It was indeed beautiful, milky white and delicate looking, with a cup-shaped lip that spread out into two long curving lobes that reminded me of trellises on a wedding dress. Dewdrops shimmered in the sunlight. "That flower is something special," I admitted. "Just stunning. I've been looking for it as well."

"And at night, it emits a heavenly scent like none other," he continued, "but I can no longer smell. I am cursed, I tell you. Cursed."

I gazed into the orchid's center at what appeared to be a face. I couldn't decide if the orchid resembled a dancing fairy, or a queen on a throne, the queen of Fakahatchee. Equally amazing was how the ghost orchid blossom appeared to be suspended in air, like an apparition. The plant has no leaves, I knew, and it does not grow in soil, only on trees. Its roots obtain everything it needs from the air. And it smells strongest at night in order to attract the giant sphinx moth, perhaps the only creature that can pollinate the orchid's deep center.

I pulled out my camera and leaned forward to take a photo.

"No," the mysterious man cried. "It's mine! I must have it!" Before I could stop him, the man lunged toward the orchid. A glint shone in his eyes, one I had only seen in people addicted to drugs or alcohol. But when he tried to grab the flower, the orchid simply vanished. He grasped at air!

"Arrgh!" the man wailed. "Not again. Not again!" And with that he began to weep. "This has been my curse—I can never have the ghost orchid."

I couldn't resist giving a short lecture. "Maybe you should just admire it, not try to possess it," I suggested.

He glared at me. "You don't know what it's like. I just have to have it. I've been all over the world collecting orchids. Nothing stands in my way. I've fought headhunters, fierce Indians, rival collectors, lawmen. Nothing has stopped me, except for this, this beautiful orchid. Oh the pain, the pain!"

He moaned loudly again. "I am cursed," he said, "cursed for all time by that mad witch doctor in Indonesia. Just because I shot his brother."

Just then the ghost orchid briefly reappeared as if to torture him further. "Oh, it's so beautiful," he said again. "So beautiful."

I realized then that I was not talking to a real man, but a ghost. My words couldn't help him. So, I left him there—the cursed orchid hunter and his unreachable prize. I didn't even take a photograph. His unearthly moans haunted me all the way to my car, and occasionally still, in nightmares.

Large vine-wrapped tree in Fakahatchee Strand State Preserve.

**A hiker wades through the swamp in Fakahatchee Strand State Preserve.**

## AUTHOR'S NOTES

In 1993, four men were arrested in Southwest Florida's Fakahatchee Strand for illegally collecting wild orchids. At the time, their haul of more than one hundred rare orchids, including three ghost orchids, was worth more than $3,000 on the black market. The case brought a great deal of publicity and inspired Susan Orlean to write *The Orchid Thief* (1998). While most people recognize the importance of protecting wild orchids today, lest these beautiful plants become extinct in the wild, orchid poaching still occurs, especially in remote areas such as Fakahatchee Strand.

Removing orchids from their natural habitat has been occurring for a long time. As mentioned in the story, collectors during the 1800s searched remote corners of the world for rare specimens. Orchid fever was like gold fever; both destructive and addicting. Collectors willing to pay top money for unusual varieties fueled the orchid craze. As species became scarce and laws were enacted, collecting wild orchids slowed down, but not entirely.

Other flowering plants in Fakahatchee Strand and South Florida, such as bromeliads, are being threatened by another culprit—Mexican weevils.

Believed to have been accidentally introduced in Florida through Mexican bromeliad shipments in the late 1980s, the weevil has already ravaged bromeliads in Myakka River State Park, Highlands Hammock State Park, and Savannahs Preserve State Park. Mexican weevils were first documented to be infesting bromeliads in Fakahatchee Strand in 2002. Researchers are looking for biological controls of the weevils and volunteers are collecting bromeliad seeds in order to replant devastated areas.

"The Ghost Orchid Ghost" was inspired by my own trips into Fakahatchee Strand and by a deep concern for the survival of rare plants, especially the famed ghost orchid.

## MORE ABOUT ORCHIDS

Orchids first appeared about 120 million years ago, when dinosaurs ruled the land. As the earth underwent radical changes, and numerous animal species died out, orchids flourished and expanded. Today, thirty-five thousand different species of orchids can be found, growing on all continents except Antarctica. In addition, orchid growers have developed about two hundred thousand hybrids.

Most of the Fakahatchee Strand's forty-four native species of orchids, including the ghost orchid, grow on trees and tree bark. These orchids are known as epiphytes, meaning they derive most of what they need from the air. The tree is simply a stable surface in which to grow.

Many native orchids are small and often go unnoticed when not in bloom. They need very specific conditions in order to survive and cannot always be successfully relocated. Tree cutting and the draining of swamps have likely caused the biggest decline of orchids in the wild.

Historically, orchids were used for medicines. Their roots were believed to be capable of curing various illnesses and sexual problems. The seedpods of one orchid, *Vanilla planifolia*, are used to flavor ice cream. The word orchid comes from *orchis*, the Latin name for testicle.

To learn more, contact groups such as the American Orchid Society, founded in 1921 to conserve orchids and their habitats. Check for orchid clubs, growers, and nurseries in your area.

## STORYTELLING TIPS

Since there are two characters in the story, try to change voices as you switch from one speaker to the other. The hiker is relatively cool and calm, but the crazed orchid collector is desperate and anguished by his curse. His voice should reflect his state of mind. Pretend you are reaching for an orchid that disappears. Ball up your fist in frustration and let out a howl. Let the audience feel his pain.

As an example of an orchid, you can borrow or purchase a domestic variety and show your audience its beauty. Many are now available in nurseries and even supermarkets. In Florida, orchids are primarily raised by commercial growers around Miami, Homestead, Orlando, and Apopka.

**Estimated Telling Time:** 7–8 minutes

# · 3 ·

# Skunk Ape Magic

$\mathcal{V}$isiting Big Cypress Swamp a few years ago, I passed a curious place in the tiny town of Ochopee—the Skunk Ape Research Headquarters. Primarily a zoo with snakes, lizards, alligators, and goats, a fellow there whom I shall call Amos was eager to share his collection of yellowed newspaper clippings and fuzzy photos that focused on "the skunk ape."

"It's real," he said, wide-eyed. "I've seen him—seven, maybe eight feet tall. Hair all over his body, and smelly, really smelly, like skunk odor mixed with swamp gas. That's because he hangs out in sulfurous alligator caves."

Amos didn't exactly smell like roses either. Sweat covered half his shirt; he looked as though he needed a shave, haircut, and a good scrubbing. He said he had been out all night looking for skunk apes. He had strung apples in one spot, he said, because "they like apples." He also laid out a trail of lima beans.

I was skeptical about the skunk ape. This was Florida's answer to Sasquatch, the Abominable Snowman, the Yeti, Big Foot, and *The Planet of the Apes*. The stories first surfaced in the 1970s, and enough new sightings are periodically reported to keep the legend alive. I wondered if the creature was made up in order to attract more tourists to the Sunshine State.

Amos showed me a recent newspaper account that featured interviews with British tourists who had been riding in a tour bus. They claimed to have seen the skunk ape lumbering through the Big Cypress Swamp. More fuzzy photos were produced. Most likely a man in a gorilla suit, I thought, maybe even Amos. I glanced at a back room to see if a furry outfit was hanging somewhere.

"So, how come no one has found bones of the skunk ape," I asked Amos, my voice dripping with skepticism.

**The wet wilderness of Big Cypress Swamp.**

"Because this is a big swamp," he said. "Things just disappear. And if the government found any bones, you think they'd tell us? They'd hide 'em like they did those UFOs that crashed in the desert."

"Panthers are rare," I countered, "and they get killed by cars and trucks. Why don't skunk apes get killed on the road?"

"Oh, they're too smart for that. They're very intelligent creatures, almost like humans. The Seminoles and Miccosukees know all about them, but they won't say much."

And so the conversation went. Amos had an answer for every question, and I soon became bored at not stumping the skunk ape expert. Perhaps it was time to play along. After all, Florida's all about make-believe worlds, something we call theme parks.

I forked over five bucks to further Amos' research, bought a skunk ape baseball cap, and left to see my friend Charlie Billie. Charlie lives in one of the many Miccosukee Indian villages along the Tamiami Trail. They call their houses "chickees." They are framed out of cypress poles and the roofs are made from thatch layered tightly together to keep out precipitation. The sides are usually open to allow for ventilation in the hot climate.

The chickees of Charlie's family were like those used by his ancestors in the early 1800s—with a few exceptions. For example, Charlie's chickee had a satellite dish atop the roof so he could get better reception on his color television. He also had a telephone and electric lights.

Charlie introduced me to family members, all of whom were friendly and rather shy. Before we walked to the far side of the camp, however, Charlie whispered a warning: "Don't eat Grandma Susie's sofkee." It was an unusual thing for him to say. Sofkee is a traditional corn soup that tastes like soupy grits, a dish frequently offered to guests as a courtesy.

"Why?" I asked.

"Let's just say Grandma Susie is getting on in years. She puts herbs in her sofkee by mistake that are old and powerful medicines. Things can happen."

"Like what?"

"You don't want to know."

I shrugged my shoulders. Was Charlie just being superstitious?

Grandma Susie was a small gray-haired woman with a sweet smile. She was rumored to be more than one hundred years old, but no one knew her exact age. She carried more knowledge about traditional Seminole medicinal herbs that anyone alive. When she saw me, her dark eyes twinkled, and she thrust a wooden spoon and a warm bowl of sofkee into my hands. She nodded, urging me to eat. She didn't speak English. Charlie rolled his eyes when I not only consumed this serving, but another as well. It tasted wonderful!

Walking back to Charlie's chickee afterward, I told him I felt great; there was no need to worry. "That's what they all say," he said, sighing. He showed me a jungle hammock where I could bed down for the night. Protected by mosquito netting, I fell asleep to the buzz of flying insects and the sound of a late-night basketball game on Charlie's television.

At one point during the night, I'm not exactly sure when, I awakened. I couldn't figure out why my feet were sticking out the end of the hammock. I moved aside the netting, stepped down, stood up, and bumped my head on a cypress rafter. That was odd. I could have sworn the rafters were more than seven feet off the ground.

Looking out over the camp scene, everything glowed in an eerie green light. Though it was night, details of buildings were clear, and distant cypress trees and sawgrass stood out. I felt a sudden urge to wander, to be part of the swamp and every living thing, from alligators to skunks. I touched my face and arms and felt thick mats of hair. That's when I leapt into the night and let out a piercing howl.

The next thing I remember was waking up in Charlie's chickee. A school bus was dropping off children along the highway. How late was it? I wondered. I realized I was naked except for a sheet that covered me, and I had a strong craving for apples.

Charlie looked at me and shook his head. "Told you not to eat Grandma Susie's sofkee."

## AUTHOR'S NOTES

"Skunk Ape Magic" was inspired by reading eyewitness accounts of Florida's skunk ape, not by actual personal encounters. The Skunk Ape Research Headquarters in Ochopee actually exists, although personalities depicted in the story have been fictionalized. Over the years I have befriended Seminole, Miccosukee ,and Muscogee Creek Indians and learned various aspects of their culture. Is there a connection between the skunk ape and Florida's native people? Do skunk apes exist in Florida? Find out by leaving a trail of lima beans, hanging apples in a tree, and keeping an all-night vigil.

## MORE ABOUT FLORIDA'S
## SEMINOLE AND MICCOSUKEE INDIAN CULTURE

Seminole and Miccosukee Indians fled to the Everglades region of South Florida in the 1830s and 1840s during the Second Seminole War (1835–1842). The remote islands and vast sawgrass and cypress expanses enabled a small group to hide and escape death or removal to Oklahoma. A formal surrender was never signed, and in the mid-1900s the US government finally recognized tribal sovereignty. The Miccosukees and Seminoles now have their own legal constitutions and elected tribal councils and chairmen.

The Florida Seminoles, numbering more than three thousand, maintain six reservations: Big Cypress, Brighton, Hollywood, Immokalee, Tampa, and Fort Pierce. Groups of independent Seminoles live off the reservations. The Miccosukees live primarily on lands along the Tamiami Trail and number more than six hundred. Although modern Seminole and Miccosukee Indian "chickee" villages still exist in South Florida, most have electricity and modern conveniences. The majority of Florida's American Indians live in conventional-style houses and work regular jobs while still retaining elements of their traditional culture and beliefs, such as clan kinships.

The Seminoles and Miccosukees are divided into clans that include wind, deer, panther, bear, otter, snake, frog, and bird. A person is born into their mother's clan. Traditionally, young people must marry someone from a different clan other than their own. People from the same clan are considered to be related, descended from a common ancestor.

Seminoles and Miccosukees share many of the same customs and tribal art forms. Both groups originally broke off from tribes of the Muscogee Creek Confederation, which were primarily located in Alabama and Georgia. Upper Creeks mostly spoke the Muscogee language, while lower Creeks spoke

Hitchiti, commonly referred to as Mikasuki. These languages are still spoken today.

Seminoles and Miccosukees are renowned for their colorful patchwork clothing, made popular when the sewing machine was introduced in Florida in the late 1800s. The two tribes have prospered in recent years, earning income from bingo, cigarette sales, tourism, and from raising cattle and catfish.

## STORYTELLING TIPS

Begin your telling of "Skunk Ape Magic" with a sense of doubt and cynicism as you describe Florida's skunk ape legends, but as the sofkee concoction takes effect, stand up, puff out your chest, and spread your arms like a huge grizzly bear stretching. You are becoming the skunk ape. Add to the story's charm by emitting an unpleasant skunk-like or sulfurous odor.

**Estimated Telling Time:** 7–8 minutes

# • 4 •

# The Wild Man of Ocheesee Swamp

*Inspired by a true story from the summer of 1884.*

Irvin wasn't quite sure when the wildness began. Perhaps it was in the battle itself when a bullet seared through his leg and then shrapnel from an exploding cannonball entered his skull. He struggled for life in a primitive field hospital at Chickamauga in 1863. His body survived the surgeries and fevers, but not his mind, and no one seemed to care when he wandered off after three months, wandered away from what was left of the bloody Civil War, no longer capable of being a soldier.

He generally walked in a southerly direction, through his land of Dixie, scouring for vegetables in farm fields and foraging on berries and roots. He was scarred in every way and avoided humans whenever possible. Months, and even years, passed. Family became a vague dream. Faces, names, and familiar places faded; he knew not how to find them, and slowly he forgot. Eventually, even his own name escaped him, along with words. And when the last of his clothes tore away from him, he did nothing to replace them, and dark hair began to grow in all places of his body. When his boots fell away, his feet became as tough as bear paws.

Perhaps the moment he knew he had crossed into being a wild animal was when he came upon an old plantation house at dusk thinking it abandoned. A large bulldog came after him and upon being confronted with the snarling beast, something took hold of him. He snarled back. Then, he reared up with claw-like fingernails and bared his teeth. This was followed by a guttural scream that sent the dog running. Afterward, he was less afraid of wild beasts, and they generally gave him space. He could howl like the wolves that roamed the forests and could scream nearly as loud as a wildcat. Yet, he could also be gentle. Once, he found a hidden fawn. He sat and stroked it for a spell and left it unharmed.

He wrestled with a playful bear cub one spring but knew enough to back away when mother bear rushed out from the brush. He learned from watching bears. Most of what they ate, he could eat. He could even catch fish with his bare hands or spear them with his fingernails and slice them open to eat the meat.

His closest call with death came when he tried to cross a swollen stream and was swept downstream. Upon emerging onto shore, gasping for breath and his vision blurry, a coiled water moccasin struck him on the hand and caused a burning pain much like the Yankee bullet years before. His hand and arm became purple and swollen and he was delirious for days.

He lived in a cave for a spell, a sheltered place with clean water and a near constant temperature. By the blackened ceilings and chipped stone, he knew native people had once lived there for generations. His dreams were the most vivid then. During sleep, he roamed with the spirits of the former occupants—watched their ways, heard their stories, saw how they lived and died. He felt kinship, but one day a wagon pulled up and men began unloading supplies for a whiskey still. He had to wait until dark to slip past and continue his wandering.

Deep in the forest, he once encountered a Muscogee Indian elder, someone nearly as secretive as him. The man started chanting when he saw him and slowly backed away, but not before leaving food and tobacco as a type of offering to a living and breathing mythological creature.

The longer the wild man roamed, the more he sought a place where no humans lived. When he reached the vast cypress forests of Ocheesee Swamp in North Florida, he stopped his roaming and moved from island to island in search of food and a feeling of peace. Here he felt safe. Here was home. Still, hunger pangs frequently wracked his body, always hunger. Gnawing from inside.

Eventually, he was spotted by some of the pioneer settlers who lived on the outskirts, and many heard his anguished cries at night. Men formed a team to find him, many of whom had served in the Confederate Army. They came with guns, ropes, and dogs, moving from island to island until they surrounded him and closed in with screams and yells. They seemed afraid of him as he snarled and howled and thrashed at them with his long fingernails. But they did not shoot. Instead, they snared him with ropes and dragged him through the swamp, afraid to touch or get close, and once on land they caged him as they would a prized hog and gazed at him with a combination of fear and fascination, wondering who he was or what he was. A skunk ape, some said, a Sasquatch. The missing link. He couldn't be a man. No man could turn into such an animal. The mere idea seemed to frighten them, that people might not be so far removed from wild animals, that it could take just take a few

**The thick cypress forest found in Ocheesee Swamp.**

years and hair would cover the body and fingernails would become claws and a species so proud of their forward evolution could revert back to something before organized civilization.

When adults weren't looking, children poked him with sticks, and when he howled at them, they ran in fear, only to be pulled back for more, drawn in by the mystery and prodded by the dares of friends.

The people gave him food and water as they would a dog. They talked and pointed, and whiskey jugs were passed around. "We got us a real skunk ape!" exalted Zeke, one of the searchers. "We're all going to be famous!"

Becky, his wife, wasn't so convinced. She approached the cage and scrunched up her nose. "But what if he's not?"

"What do mean, woman?"

"I mean just that, what if he's not? I been thinking real hard on it, and doing some praying. What if he was born to a God-fearing Christian family and somehow got that way, maybe in the war?"

"No, couldn't be! You're just trying to ruin our excitement."

Becky scrunched up her nose again and looked closer at the creature thrashing about in the cage. "It could be. It just could be."

Zeke's mood sobered quickly. "Maybe we should have just shot him and buried him in the swamp."

"Might have been the merciful thing to do, all right. But if he is a man, he got that way somehow and maybe he can go back to being a civilized man." She glanced at Zeke and snickered, and decided not to say more, but the question gnawed at her. What if . . .

Zeke gulped whiskey from a nearby jug as Becky walked away. "No way he's a man," he muttered. "No way a man could get like that. That's a skunk ape. The first ever captured skunk ape. We're all going to be famous." But his enthusiasm had faded, doubt creeping in like swamp water.

Eventually, they put his caged body in a wagon and took him to the state mental hospital in nearby Chattahoochee to see if the creature was really a mad man who had escaped, but there was no record of an escapee. He was then taken to Tallahassee where more fancy dressed doctors pointed and wondered. "The teeth," said one, "we must see the teeth." Four men held down the creature and after several attempts, the doctor examined his teeth, or the few that remained in his mouth. "Those are not the teeth of an animal!" he announced, finally. "This is a man, a mad man." Wires were sent to mental hospitals in other states; responses came in. No escapees matched the description.

Word spread of the wild man. Dispatches were sent through Florida, Georgia, and Alabama, but since the wild man did not talk and had no belongings, details remained sketchy.

Eventually, the wild man was sent back to the state mental hospital in Chattahoochee where his screams and cries were considered strange even by those who had been sent there for being mad. Orderlies held him and shaved his face, cut his hair, bathed and clothed him, and trimmed his nails as much

Old homestead along the edge of Ocheesee Swamp.

for their own protection as appearance. And as the wild man ate regular food and was confined indoors, and heard the talk of humans, he slowly began to resemble a man again. During a dream, a voice called to him as if from a distant cloud, a woman's voice, one very familiar—perhaps his mother's. "Irvin," she said over and over, "Irvin." So one day, instead of screams, he uttered the one word he knew. After that, the orderlies and doctors no longer called him The Wild Man of Ocheesee Swamp, but Irvin. The man who had once lived as an animal, the man who could only speak his name.

## AUTHOR'S NOTES

Not much is known about the wild man other than the stories told in Jackson County and news accounts from the time, such as this one in *The New York Times* in August of 1884: "News brought by the steamer Amos Hays from Lower River is to the effect that the wild man captured in Ocheecee Swamp, near Chattahoochee, and carried to Tallahassee, did not belong to a Florida asylum, and that all inquiry proved unavailing to identify him. He had been swimming in Ocheecee Lake, from island to island, and when taken was entirely destitute of clothing, emaciated and covered with a phenomenal growth of hair."

Ocheesee was spelled different then, and the open areas of the cypress swamp are sometimes referred to as a pond or lake today. This story is my attempt to fill in the gaps and to relay how the "wild man" became wild, and what happened to him. If you have ever been on a boat or kayak in Ocheesee Swamp, you will quickly realize how extensive and thick it is with cypress trees, even too thick to move through in places, and you had better be careful not to get lost. Fortunately, a five-mile paddling loop trail has been marked on cypress trees by county officials to make navigation easier and safer.

Many thanks to Dale Jackson, noted historian from Jackson County, for uncovering the original news story of the wild man in *The New York Times* and publishing it in his blog.

## STORYTELLING TIPS

During the dialogue between Becky and Zeke about whether the wild man is a skunk ape or not, show a lot of enthusiasm in Zeke's voice at first as he thinks they captured a skunk ape, but quickly drop that enthusiasm the more Becky talks.

**Estimated Telling Time:** 8–9 minutes

# • 5 •

# Swamp Shadow

*M*ichelle knew something was following her. She felt it soon after embarking on the Florida National Scenic Trail from its southern terminus in the remote Big Cypress Swamp.

Being from Pennsylvania, Michelle had read about the 1,300-mile hiking trail across Florida. She enjoyed backpacking in the Pocono Mountains and other areas of Pennsylvania, but snow and ice limited her opportunities in winter. So, she had earned money painting houses in order to hike up to four months through the Florida wilds, beginning in December. She had never been to Florida, never seen a cypress tree or swamp before her flight to Fort Myers. Now, she was on her way, but she immediately questioned her decision. Water covered the footpath; the dry season was late in arriving. She even spotted small fish swimming in the pools of water on the trail! But fish were the least of her worries. Something was following her.

*Slosh, slosh, slosh.* There was no way she could move quietly through water with a full backpack, so occasionally she'd stop and listen. She heard nothing. At one point, she abruptly turned and scanned the dwarf cypress forest behind her, and the growing afternoon shadows. "Who's out there?" she yelled. "Why are you following me?" Nothing. No one answered. A blue heron squawked and flew up from a nearby marsh.

Michelle scrunched up her face, trying to think. Was it just nerves or was something or someone actually there? She felt a pressing against the back of her head, a primitive warning, it seemed. She yearned for her faithful hiking companion, Max, a German shepherd, but she had heard how alligators are often drawn to dogs in swamps and along waterways, so she left him with friends. Interestingly, in several muddy spots Michelle spotted animal prints about the size and shape of Max's, maybe even larger. She seemed to be following the animal, whatever it was.

The wet path of the Florida National Scenic Trail in Big Cypress Swamp.

**Panther tracks near Big Cypress Swamp.**

Michelle continued her hike. The same feeling of being followed returned. It was even stronger this time. She whirled around. Something moved in the dim light. She had no doubt now. "Who are you?" she called. "Come out where I can see you!" She waited. Nothing happened. It was as if she were being tracked by a shadow.

Michelle sighed, turned, and hiked some more. She gripped her walking stick tighter and pulled out a can of pepper spray. *Don't panic*, she told herself—she had been trained in self-defense—but several thoughts raced through her head. What if her follower wasn't a real person? What if it was a ghost or, even worse, what if death was stalking her, the shadow of death? She had heard a story about that when she was a child in summer camp. Could it be true? Why did it choose her? At twenty-eight, she was too young to die.

The campsite was on dry ground in a grove of pine trees. That was a relief. Michelle immediately gathered sticks, started a cheery fire, and stripped off soggy boots and socks. The constant hiking in water had softened her feet, causing several small blisters to form. This was not the ideal first day on the trail. At least the shadow seemed to retreat once the fire got going. She felt better about that. She had often hiked alone, rarely getting spooked, but she had never been in such an unfamiliar environment.

Just when darkness set in, Michelle set up a tent and spread out her sleeping bag. Then, a scream! The first of many blood-curling screams echoed through the forest. She felt the hair prickle on the back of her neck. With a shaking hand, Michelle pulled out her thumb-sized flashlight and shined it in the direction of the scream. She heard no movement, but eventually, the tiny light illuminated two yellow eyes about three feet off the ground. That's when she heard another scream from the opposite end of her camp, just as shrill and disturbing as the first. She whirled and shined her beam on two more yellow eyes. Screams now arose from both sides simultaneously. Any moment she felt she would be pounced upon by these fierce swamp beasts, whatever they were. She clutched her walking stick and waited.

The screaming animals drew closer together. Michelle shined her light. The beam caught a blur of tan fur as two large Florida panthers leapt toward each other in a snarling battle. It was like a fight between housecats, only twenty times more ferocious. The cats slashed and bit. Fur, dirt, and pine needles flew in the air. Each panther attempted to bite the skull or neck of the other, an instant deathblow. Finally, the smaller cat backed away into a clump of palmettos and then leaped away in retreat. The other pursued in darkness. Briefly, Michelle heard the two animals running through the swamp, and then only cicadas and tree frogs. She shivered. Her heart was still racing. She witnessed something very few humans had seen before—a fight over territory between two male Florida panthers.

**Swimming panther at the Tallahassee Museum.**

Michelle thought about hiking out of the trail in the morning and flying back to Pennsylvania. No one would blame her, if they believed her story—a woman out alone with wild beasts. Then she smiled. "Not!" she said to herself. This was exciting, far better than painting solid colors on house walls. She realized she had never been in any real danger. One panther was tracking the other and she had been caught in the middle.

She glanced up at the incredible spread of the Milky Way. Her eyes followed a shooting star as it streaked across the northern horizon. She would continue her journey through the swamp and beyond and see if other adventures could possibly match this one.

## AUTHOR'S NOTES

"Swamp Shadow" was inspired by a memorable period in 2003 when I accompanied biologists in the Big Cypress Swamp region during their ongoing studies of the Florida panther. I learned how silent and swift panthers can travel in pursuit or flight, and how easily they can hide. About the only way to find the elusive cat is to use specially trained hounds that will track and chase one up a tree.

On the third day with the biologists, we found a dead female panther that had lost her life as she defended her cubs from an aggressive male panther. Studying the body and trampled plants around her, I tried to imagine the fight between two adult panthers—piercing screams, tense posturing, tawny bodies crashing into palmetto and brush, lightning quick thrusts with razor-sharp claws. The deathblow in this case was a bite to the skull. This experience, along with a hike I made on the Florida National Scenic Trail through Big Cypress Swamp during flood stage, helped me create "Swamp Shadow."

## MORE ABOUT THE FLORIDA PANTHER

When thinking about the Florida panther today, an image of the Everglades immediately comes to the mind of many. That's because most panthers are now found south of Lake Okeechobee in the Big Cypress/Everglades region of Florida. It wasn't always the case. Florida's big cats were once widely distributed throughout the Southeast, being one of more than twenty subspecies of cougars. The Everglades/Big Cypress region is not necessarily prime habitat for the panther, but it is the largest chunk of relatively undisturbed wilderness remaining in its former domain.

The good news is that panther numbers are rising. From an estimated low of 30–50 in 1995, according to the U.S. Fish and Wildlife Service researchers now believe there could be 120–230 Florida panthers living in the wild. The big challenge continues to be preserving panther habitats into the future. South Florida panthers are being hemmed in by development, so researchers are seeking to establish another panther stronghold in the Southeast to ensure the species' survival.

One hurdle has always been the panthers' requirement for huge territories. Male panthers roam more than 150–450 square miles; female panthers about 60–100 square miles. Male panther home ranges rarely overlap with each other. Otherwise, a fight could erupt, especially during mating season. On rare occasions, a female panther will have to defend her cubs from an aggressive male.

Female panthers have one to four kittens. Young panthers stay with their mother up to two years; the mother teaches them how to hunt and defends them from threats. An individual panther needs to kill a deer or wild hog every seven to ten days to remain healthy, but a female with young may kill one every three days. The energy expended to catch smaller animals such as raccoons and armadillos can sometimes sustain an individual panther, but it cannot fulfill the energy needs of a nursing mother. For this reason, the availability of large prey animals such as deer and wild hogs in panther habitats is critical to their survival.

Florida panthers have a remarkable sense of balance that enables them to climb trees and leap and twist through the air. They are renowned for their jumping ability, both in terms of distance and height. Their claws stay sharp for climbing and attacking prey because they can be retracted when on the move. Panthers generally hunt at night. During the daylight, their eyesight is about the same as ours, but their nighttime vision is far superior.

Florida panthers differ from their western counterparts in several ways. They are generally darker in color (tawny or reddish brown), smaller in body size, and have different skull dimensions than other subspecies. White flecks from repeated tick bites dot the back of the neck and shoulders, a swirl or cowlick can be found in the back of the neck, and the long tail often has a crook or kink at the end. Some of these traits may be the result of inbreeding within a small population. There has never been a documented report of a black Florida panther.

According to panther biologists, several measures have contributed to the survivability of panthers. They include the introduction of the Texas cougar, the Florida panthers' closest cousin. These cougars have strengthened the gene pool for panthers. Wildlife crossings and adjacent right-of-way fencing has also proven effective, projects that need to extend to more South Florida highways as panthers expand their habitat base.

The key to panther recovery is public support and proper funding for research, management efforts, habitat restoration and protection, and reintroduction efforts.

## STORYTELLING TIPS

Since "Swamp Shadow" has no dialogue except for one person yelling at something or someone whom she believes is following her, you can build up suspense by doing just that. Pretend you are walking and abruptly turn around and scream, "Why are you following me?" If you see your audience jump, you know you've got their full attention. Good storytellers are also good actors.

During the scene where the hiker is at her camp and she shines a flashlight at the source of the scream, you can pull out a dim pocket flashlight and shine it into a dark area, showing how little light it gives off. As with many of the stories, a darkened room or a nighttime campfire setting is helpful.

**Estimated Telling Time:** 7–8 minutes

## · *6* ·

# Mosquito Crazy

*R*alph's specialty as a biologist was extracting blood and other fluids from animals and studying them in a laboratory. He would travel around the country at different times, helping with wildlife studies, but his least favorite assignment was working in the mangrove swamps near Florida Bay in Everglades National Park, studying the endangered American crocodile. It wasn't the large reptiles that bothered Ralph—they rarely attacked people. It was the ravenous clouds of mosquitoes.

Everglades National Park boasts more than thirty different kinds of mosquitoes. Some prefer specific environments such as thick mangrove swamps or wide expanses of sawgrass swamps. But at any given time, in any type of environment in the Everglades, one or more species of mosquitoes are feeding, especially during warm weather, which was most of the time. Ralph could never get used to them. None of the repellents he tried were completely effective. He would sweat off bug dope about as quickly as he sprayed it on.

Ralph and his coworkers worked out of the tiny town of Flamingo, which is situated at the tip of the Everglades. Historically, people who lived in Flamingo had a difficult time. In 1893, one naturalist reported that a cloud of mosquitoes was so thick they extinguished an oil lamp.

Flamingo's remoteness and infamous mosquitoes kept away all but the hardiest of pioneers. The town, named in 1893 for the colorful flamingo birds that once arrived in great numbers from Cuba and the Bahamas (rarely seen today), was historically a handful of rustic houses built on pilings. Interior walls were covered with thick soot because residents constantly kept wood smoldering in smudge pots to keep away mosquitoes. Even baby carriages were said to have smoldering smudge pots underneath them.

**A calm evening with no wind along Florida Bay may mean more mosquitoes.**

When a scarcely passable road was built to Flamingo in 1922, one resident joked, "There were fewer people than ever at Flamingo. They had found a way to get out."

Ralph believed all the stories. He didn't want to be there but he had a job to do. Every evening, he climbed into a boat with three other biologists and searched for crocodiles. They would capture, weigh, measure, and tag the thrashing creatures while Ralph took blood samples. All the while, Ralph would be spitting out mosquitoes that had flown into his mouth, wiping them from his eyes, and slapping them from his ears. One night, he had had enough. Crazily, be began flailing his arms. "I can't take it anymore!" he screamed. He leaped overboard. Several crocodiles moved away, but not too far. Ralph's coworkers quickly caught him and dragged him out of the water, wrapping him in a plastic tarp; it served as a type of straitjacket. Ralph screamed the whole time. "I hate mosquitoes!" he cried. "No more! No more!"

Back at Flamingo, Ralph's coworkers agreed he should take a few days off. The study was almost finished, just two or three more trips into the mangrove swamp. Ralph was tempted to quit but he couldn't let the team down. His expertise was needed. He vowed to finish the study.

When Ralph returned the following week, he seemed like a different person. He was calm and polite, and he apologized for his behavior during the previous outing. "I have been working on a new repellent," he announced. "I've made it from the fluid of mosquitoes, and I have injected it under my skin. It works better than anything else. You'll see."

It didn't take long for the test to begin. Mosquitoes soon swarmed the group. While his coworkers swatted and waved at mosquitoes, Ralph wasn't bothered a bit by the pesky creatures. He sat calmly in the boat, enjoying the maze of winding creeks that penetrated the thick mangrove swamp. Near sunset, however, when mosquitoes were normally the worst, Ralph started acting weird. He had trouble sitting up or holding up his head. He suddenly began squirming on the bottom of the boat, making loud peeping noises. Before anyone knew what was happening, he slithered overboard, snake-like, into the dark water. His coworkers frantically searched with flashlights and called his name, but they never saw Ralph again.

Later that month, a group of Cuban refugees landed near Flamingo in a raft. They had floated and paddled all the way from Cuba to escape communism. The men and women spoke rapidly in Spanish and only one person in town could understand them. The tale, as it was translated, told of a giant mosquito the size of a man, flying in and out of a cloud of regular-sized mosquitoes. It didn't bite them, fortunately, because they guessed it was a male mosquito, and most people know that male mosquitoes don't bite.

## AUTHOR'S NOTES

I've had the good fortune of exploring Florida Bay and adjacent swamps by boat and on foot. A main drawback of my time spent there was a pesky little creature known as the mosquito. The area is likely the mosquito capital of Florida, if not the world, especially during the warm months—which means most of the year in South Florida. If hiking by land, I've often found myself running to escape clouds of hungry mosquitoes. On the water, I try to paddle faster, moving into open water and praying for a stiff breeze. Thus, it was no surprise when I heard that mosquitoes drove a field biologist so crazy, coworkers had to wrap him in a tarp to restrain him. Thus, the seeds for "Mosquito Crazy" were planted.

While swatting or running from mosquitoes, it is important to keep in mind that mosquitoes are a vital part of the Everglades food chain since so many birds, fish, and other insects feed on mosquitoes or their larvae.

**Florida Bay evening.**

## MORE ABOUT AMERICAN CROCODILES AND FLORIDA BAY

Few people realize that crocodiles are not restricted to remote African jungles and *Tarzan* movies. The American crocodile (*Crocodylus acutus*) is found in Florida. Highly endangered, an estimated five hundred to one thousand wild American crocodiles live in the southern tip of the Florida Peninsula and around Key Largo. They are also found in parts of the Caribbean and Central and South America, although their population outside of the United States is highly fragmented and vulnerable to extinction.

Crocodiles differ from alligators in that their snouts are more pointed, and their skin is grayer. Crocodiles can also grow larger than alligators if they live long enough. The largest recorded specimen was fifteen feet, captured in the 1800s, although tales of larger crocodiles abound. Mating generally occurs in late winter and early spring, with nesting in late April or early May.

To view crocodiles, visit Florida Bay, the adjacent Ten Thousand Islands, and northern Key Largo, but keep a safe distance. Infrequent sightings of crocodiles have occurred as far north as Tampa Bay. Scientists believe that crocodiles, especially juveniles, are good barometers of an ecosystem's health. If this is true, the Everglades restoration plan may be good news for American crocodiles since Florida Bay, the crocodiles' main habitat, is part of the Everglades system.

Florida Bay, situated at the very bottom of the Florida mainland and the Florida keys, is unlike any estuary in the United States. At twenty-five by forty miles in size, it is huge, yet an NBA basketball center could wade its entire length without getting his nose wet. Its tropical waters are not dominated by a large freshwater river, like Apalachicola Bay or the Chesapeake. Fresh water primarily flows in from sloughs connected to the wide "river of grass" just to the north.

Because the hydrology of the Everglades system has been severely altered by canals, development, and farms, Florida Bay has been starved of vital fresh water—a 70 percent decline by one estimate. It is, for the most part, too salty, and fresh water often flows in at the wrong time of year. Many of its native life forms have suffered. Seagrass die-offs, algae blooms, and fish kills blemish its recent past.

Besides the American crocodile, Florida Bay's native wildlife includes bald eagles, loggerhead sea turtles, sawfish, and other threatened and endangered species. It is, like the "river of grass," one of Florida's unique ecological treasures.

What is the future of Florida Bay? No one claims to have all the answers. Most researchers agree, however, that an increase in clean fresh water delivered at the right time of year will produce beneficial results.

## STORYTELLING TIPS

When telling "Mosquito Crazy," you may want to practice your "*bzzzzzz*," imitating a mosquito or lots of mosquitoes. Have your audience practice beforehand so they can "*bzzzzzz*" right along with you. Thousands of mosquitoes descending all at once is an unforgettable sound, so the more help you have with the "*bzzzzz*," the more realistic and entertaining the story will be.

**Estimated Telling Time:** 6–7 minutes

## • 7 •

# Watson's Ghost

*J*acob could kick a soccer ball and play video games as well as most ten-year-olds, but he was peculiar in one way: he could see and hear ghosts. The encounters were sometimes upsetting, but rarely frightening. What bothered Jacob more was that his friends, and especially his parents, didn't believe him.

One week during winter break Jacob's father, Tom, proposed an adventure: a canoe-camping trip through the Ten Thousand Islands in Everglades National Park. Winter was the best time to explore the area. Otherwise, mosquitoes, flies, and no-see-ums were thick and could ruin an outing.

Jacob was excited—canoe camping could be fun and challenging—but he did feel some hesitation. Were there ghosts in the Ten Thousand Islands and what were they like? Few people ask such questions, but ghosts rarely left Jacob alone. They were lost souls, wandering, searching for peace, and not knowing how to find it.

Jacob felt an all too familiar sense of dread on the drive from their home in Orlando to Everglades City, in the heart of the Ten Thousand Islands. He was reading the Everglades guidebook that described campsites on their itinerary and came to one called Watson's Place. A notorious outlaw named Ed Watson settled on an old Calusa Indian shell mound and began a farming operation. According to the book, Watson killed several people on the site, the bodies of whom were never found. The book concluded: "And if you are here by yourself, don't be surprised if the spirits of Watson's victims keep you company, whispering in the wind." Jacob shuddered.

Tom noticed the change in Jacob's expression.

"What's wrong?"

"Oh nothing."

"Come on, tell me. I've seen that look before."

"Well, this book talks about this one campsite having a lot of ghosts. Watson's Place."

"Oh come on, the author was just having a bit of fun."

Jacob fell silent. It wasn't funny to him.

"Now Jacob, don't give me that look. This trip will be great. And you'll be so tired by the time we get to Watson's Place on the first day you won't even think about ghosts. Plus, how many times do I have to tell you, there's no such thing as ghosts!"

Jacob nodded. He had heard it all before. Obviously, his father had never had ghosts calling to him from the shadows or felt cold chills rushing across his face, or experienced the heavy, unsettled feeling of being visited by a restless spirit. It was a burden he would have to bear—alone.

After receiving a permit for their five-day trip from the ranger station, father and son packed their canoe and set off across the wide Chokoloskee Bay. "It's seventeen miles to Watson's Place," Tom announced. "But I think the wind and tides will be with us most of the way."

**The front of the Smallwood's Store museum in Chokoloskee.**

After three miles, Tom steered the boat to a red tin-roofed shack on pilings in the tiny town of Chokoloskee. "This should be the Smallwood's Store," he announced. "The guidebook says Seminole Indians and early residents used to trade and buy goods here. Now, it's a museum."

They paid a small entrance fee and wandered through the wood structure, viewing exhibits and early trade items. A gray-haired woman manned the counter. "Where you headed?" she asked Jacob. "I saw you pull up in your canoe."

"Watson's Place," Jacob replied rather grimly.

"Oh yes, Ed Watson's old place," she replied. Her nod was as grim as Jacob's look.

"Did that man really kill a bunch of people?"

"That's what they say—killed his workers one by one instead of paying them—but it was hard to prove. No one ever witnessed him do any killing, or they never lived to tell. The whole bunch there were desperadoes."

"What happened to him? I mean, Mr. Watson?"

"Well, the story goes that he pulled up here at Chokoloskee one day and there was a big crowd waiting for him because they heard he had just hunted a man down and shot him. Everyone was kind of afraid of Watson, so I guess they figured they was safer in a group. Someone accused him of murdering one of his hands. When they asked for his gun, an argument started—Watson had a short temper—and Watson raised his shotgun and pressed the trigger, but it misfired. Then, the whole town opened fire on Watson. Left him with more bullet holes than you could count. One man said he never saw a man so dead. That was the end of Ed Watson. They buried him on one of the keys not far from here, but they later moved the body to Fort Myers to be near his wife's grave. Guess the townspeople then didn't want him too close, even when he was dead."

Jacob nodded. He could understand, but he knew that wouldn't stop a ghost from returning.

Even with the incoming tide helping them up the Lopez River, Jacob was bone-tired by the time they reached the high cleared mound of the Watson's Place campsite. Much to their surprise there were mosquitoes—in late December—making them wonder what the place was like in August. Swatting bugs, they pitched tents and Tom cooked them a noodle dish, typical camp fare, and they went to bed soon after sunset. Tom had been right about one thing. Jacob was too tired to think about ghosts. He went right to sleep.

Jacob awoke just before dawn. Twilight was spreading over the mangrove trees. The tide was out, exposing numerous mud banks. Blackened trunks of long dead mangroves lay exposed and twisted, like fallen bodies.

**Old boat and skins on display in the Smallwoods Store.**

Raccoons scurried along the shore in search of food. Wading birds poked about the shallows. A small alligator drifted past.

Jacob stretched stiff muscles and began to explore. As he strode across the back of the island, he felt a familiar pressing on the back of his head. Then he heard a whisper: "Go, go now." A cold hand pushed him forward.

He heard another whisper in front of him. "No, go back. You don't belong." He felt like he was in the middle of an invisible tug-of-war.

When he pushed through a small opening in the mangroves, he spotted two ghosts standing on the edge of a watery pool. They were dressed in old-time clothes, with floppy broad-rimmed hats, and one carried a handgun. They were arguing, and in the faint light their voices seemed to float on the heavy air. "I'm due my pay," said one man with a long scar on his cheek. "I've been working for you for months with nary a dime to show for it. I'm due my pay, and then I'm cutting out of here."

The other man, whom Jacob assumed was Ed Watson, poked a finger at the chest of the other. "You work till I say you're done. You're a wanted man, like all of us, and I'm giving you shelter here."

"More like prison," the other man shot back. "This place is a hellhole. The bugs alone will drive you crazy. I'll take my chances somewheres else."

The man lunged for Watson, but Watson knocked him back. "You want pay," he shouted, "I'll give you pay, just like I paid the others." With lightning quickness, he drew a six-gun and shot the man directly in the forehead. As the man fell back into the dark water, slack-jawed, the ghostly images faded, and a whistling osprey pierced the air.

Jacob heard a loud rustling sound behind him and turned to see if it was another ghost or a person. It was his father, rushing down the trail in the dim light with a sleepy-eyed look. "I thought I heard arguing," he said, puffing, "then a gunshot. And who was that guy with the floppy hat?" He hesitantly peered into the mangroves, wiping his eyes. "You okay?"

Jacob smiled. "You must have been dreaming, Dad. There's nothing here but birds and raccoons."

## AUTHOR'S NOTES

One of my earliest memories was when I was three years old in my grandparents' house and I lay awake in my crib. Suddenly, my baby rattle lifted and shook in midair, then dropped. I screamed and my parents came, but, not surprisingly, they didn't believe me. "You must have been dreaming," they said. Children can have vivid imaginations, so it's not uncommon for adults to brush off unusual stories told by young people.

This early memory, coupled with a recent kayaking trip through the famous Ten Thousand Islands, helped me to weave this tale. Plus, the main guidebook for the park warns visitors about ghosts at Watson's Place, so beware!

## MORE ABOUT THE TEN THOUSAND ISLANDS

Florida's Ten Thousand Islands are steeped in history and secrets. The area is a watery maze of mangrove forests where Calusa Indians once dug canals and built islands with their discarded shells. Seminole Indians and outlaws sought refuge along the sometimes bewildering, twisting waterways. Men once eked out a living by hunting alligators and crocodiles, killing egrets for their plumes, and making moonshine.

While the Ten Thousand Islands contained some harmless hermits, it also harbored numerous fugitives, such as Ed Watson, who allegedly killed the outlaw Belle Starr, among other people. An early account of seven unwritten laws for the area reads like something out of the frontier West:

- Suspect every man.
- Ask no questions.
- Settle your own quarrels.
- Never steal from an islander.
- Stick by him, even if you do not know him.
- Shoot quick, when your secret is in danger.
- Cover your kill.

Smallwood's Store in Chokoloskee, mentioned in the story, was where Seminole Indians and residents swapped pelts and silver money for tools, guns, and staples. Today, paddlers and other visitors can stop at the cracker-style landmark and peruse the museum and gift shop.

Environmentally, more than two hundred species of birds frequent the Ten Thousand Islands. Mangrove forests dominate the landscape, the leaves of which fall and create a rich detritus that is the base of the estuarine food web. Numerous fish, dolphins, and manatees swim the channels, bays, and coves of the area. Rich seagrass beds are nursery grounds for a variety of fish, shellfish, and crustaceans, and they also provide food for manatees and sea turtles.

## STORYTELLING TIPS

In telling this story to young people, you might want to pose the question: Have you ever seen or heard something unusual but no one else would believe you? This is a common occurrence and your audience will develop sympathy with Jacob, the lead character, as a result. A cap pistol is a good prop during the ghostly murder scene.

**Estimated Telling Time:** 9–10 minutes

# · 8 ·

# Magical Swamp Dancers

$\mathscr{I}$ was knee-deep in water and muck. The sun was dipping low, and I worried about being caught in the swamp after dark. Few feelings are worse.

The swamp slog was part of my exploration of a new piece of public property along Lake Istokpoga, one of many connected lakes below Disney World that make up the Everglades headwaters. I was writing a magazine article, but I wasn't prepared to spend the night away from my car and tent. I had a water bottle, a granola bar, bug repellent, pocketknife, and a small first-aid kit—what you might need for a day trip, not an overnight one.

As I wandered, using my compass to set a straight course, I passed scattered cypress trees. A hunter had built a crude wooden deer stand near the top of one cypress and nailed two-by-fours on the trunk for a ladder. I climbed the stand to scan my surroundings and plot the easiest way out. To the south was a small rise of tall grass and a large live oak tree. Just beyond, it looked like dry land. Feeling hopeful, I climbed down and waded toward the rise. Abruptly, a deep-throated grunt emerged from beside the live oak: "*Brrruuh!*" I froze. Mysterious grunts always have a chilling effect. "*Brrruuh!*" I heard it again.

Peering into shadows, I made out the shape of a massive dark creature, perhaps a black bear or wild boar. I hoped for a bear. If there was a dangerous critter in these woods, it would be a riled-up boar. Most Florida black bears are shy. They run away if approached, but a boar can be more aggressive.

The creature grunted louder and as it moved forward, I could see it was a boar with tusks. A dangerous animal. Slowly backing away, I glanced around for possible trees to climb and knew the deer stand would be my only way to escape.

Suddenly, without warning, the boar charged. I turned and ran as fast as I could through knee-deep water, though I felt I was running in slow mo-

**Swimming wild hog.**

tion. The boar crashed into the water behind me, snorting wildly. My worst nightmare was coming true.

Frantic, I reached the deer stand and began scrambling up. A sharp pain stabbed through my foot. The boar had gored me. I didn't stop, however, until I reached the top of the stand and sat on the platform, looking down. The huge boar circled and thrashed about, snorting and thrusting up his ugly tusks. Why should he be so upset? I wondered. I was the one trapped and hurt.

When I caught my breath and stopped shaking, I examined my foot. The tusk had slashed the side through my tennis shoe. My foot was bleeding but no arteries had been cut, fortunately. I let it bleed for a minute, then took out my first-aid kit and began bandaging the wound. This was going to be a long night.

I watched the sunset and moonrise. The grumpy boar left but I wasn't about to climb down and wander through the swamp at night. I resigned myself to spending the night in the stand. I was chilled from being wet and my foot throbbed with pain, but at least it was a warm night. And because I was many feet off the ground, mosquitoes didn't bother me much. One should look on the bright side!

I eventually dozed off leaning against the tree, but at some moment in the wee hours, faint music and singing stirred me awake. I looked out and blinked hard. I blinked again. Was I dreaming? In the small grassy rise near the live oak was a gathering of little people, each one about two feet tall, glowing in faint blue light. Most were dressed in what looked to be old-time pioneer clothes and hats, and some wore Seminole Indian clothing of bright patchwork. They were dancing in a circle, singing in high-pitched voices. I couldn't make out the words. Perhaps it was a language all their own. Occasionally, I heard giggling, like that of young children. A tinkling sound of instruments filled the air, but I saw none.

Who could they be? Where did they come from? I only had questions and no answers.

Captivated, I watched the mysterious dancing until the first glow of dawn. Then, as light penetrated the swamp and birds filled the air with their beautiful songs, the magical swamp dancers disappeared.

Carefully, I climbed down from the stand, nursing my foot, and stepped into the dark water. I worried about infection, but I had no choice. At least there were no signs of the aggressive boar.

After wading through the water, I climbed onto the rise of dry land. I stopped in amazement. Everywhere the little people had danced small flowers of many colors grew, forming a rainbow-like spiral. The ground seemed to glow too. I felt tingly all over. And then a small black object caught my eye. Reaching down, I picked up a palm-sized broad-rimmed hat. It seemed a fitting souvenir of a memorable night, but as I turned to move away, a wisp of wind kicked up and blew the hat from my hand. I watched it float away, twirling in air. Then it disappeared like the little people.

When I left the rise, another strange thing happened. I no longer limped. I peeled away the bandage to find my foot completely healed! "Thank you," I muttered, not knowing if anyone could hear. The response came in a muffled giggle from behind the oak, followed by a flash of blue light bouncing across the wet prairie.

## AUTHOR'S NOTES

The first part of this tale is true. I explored the area featured in the story along South Florida's Lake Istokpoga, now known as the Royce Tract, managed by the Florida Fish and Wildlife Conservation Commission. The Everglades headwaters are a series of connected water bodies just south of Disney World known as the Kissimmee Chain of Lakes. Protecting land along these lakes is an important step toward protecting and restoring the entire Everglades system.

The area I explored was swampier than I anticipated, made worse by a recent tropical storm. I had to wade more than hike. It was slow going and as the sun dipped below treetops, I worried about being stranded after dark. That's when I spotted a huge wild boar. From this point in the story, I delve into a bit of fiction since I did find my way out that evening without injury.

Regarding the little people, these mythical beings are part of southeastern American Indian folklore, and those of other cultures in the world. I've had my own experiences, so I guess that makes me a believer. I've never seen the little people dance, but I've heard tales, and my research uncovered one written account, which I relay in the next section.


## MORE ABOUT "THE LITTLE PEOPLE"


Little people are known to the Seminole and Muscogee Creek people as being mischievous, but also as having great power and knowledge. They come in different sizes, and some may look young while others sport long gray beards. Indian children often report playing with little people and little people are believed to have helped to find lost children.

In southeastern native culture little people are often associated with traditional healers, helping Indian doctors select suitable medicinal plants and giving the doctors special songs and chants. Some native people are very secretive about their knowledge of the little people, especially to outsiders and unbelievers. It is believed that the little people only show themselves when they want to be seen.

In the book *Life with the Little People* by Chickasaw author Robert Perry, the story of a Muscogee elder out hunting once day, who stumbles upon a dance ground of the little people, is told. He meets several little people who ask him to return for a dance. Here is what he tells happened upon his return, "The leader waved his hand, motioning for me to rest and watch. The little leader started singing his songs, 'A-E-A, A-E-A, He-Hoe, He-Hoe, A-E-A, A-E-A!' as they danced around the circle. It's kind of a prayer for people they care about. On many other nights, I came back with my dance clothes on. I would watch the little people's stomp dance far into the night. One night they did an honor dance for me. An honor dance is done for a chief, not an ordinary person such as me. It was great!"

According to the account, no one in the man's family ever became sick after the honor dance, and the elder who witnessed the little people's dance lived to be very old.

## STORYTELLING TIPS

To tell and enjoy "Magical Swamp Dancers" it is best to suspend adult logic and become more child-like. Traditional American Indian people view themselves as part of an immense multidimensional universe filled with wonder and mystery. People steeped in Western society, on the other hand, often limit their beliefs to as far as their eyes can see. Tell this story with your voice filled with awe, as if you are there watching the little people dance.

Do little people exist? That might be a question you can pose to your audience after telling the story. As a prop, you might produce a small black hat (obtained from a doll), like the one in the story.

**Estimated Telling Time:** 7–8 minutes

# · 9 ·

# Red's Island

$\mathcal{O}$ne weekend I wanted to get away for some peace and quiet. Work had been hectic and I had become weary of being confined by the four walls of my office. So I chose to paddle my kayak into Mosquito Lagoon near Titusville, a wild place of islands, creeks, and swamps protected from the Atlantic Ocean by a huge peninsula.

On Saturday morning I registered at the visitor's center of the Canaveral National Seashore and received a permit allowing me to camp on one of the remote islands. I would have no neighbors, electricity, running water, and bathroom facilities. It was just what I needed—an entire island to myself!

The island was only a couple of miles from the visitor's center, so I chose a roundabout way to get there in order to do some birdwatching. Thousands of birds migrate to Mosquito Lagoon every year since it is a major nursery area for fish and other sea life, and it produces more than its share of healthy mosquitoes and other insects.

With permit in hand, I secured my gear into my kayak and paddled a short way to Turtle Mound. This is a huge shell mound created by Timucuan Indians over a span of six hundred years. It's taller than a three-story house and after climbing to the top, I enjoyed a raptor's view of tidal creeks, marshes, and unspoiled islands. My excitement grew.

Next, I paddled to Eldora, once a thriving town where steamboats loaded and unloaded passengers and goods. When a new shipping channel was established a couple of miles away, and a railroad was built on the mainland, Eldora faded away. Only one restored house remains.

Many people once lived in Mosquito Lagoon—from American Indians to pioneers—but not so much today.

**Eldora historic home along the Mosquito Lagoon.**

I soon paddled along palm and live oak-covered islands, all uninhabited, and entered one remote cove after another. Fish darted away as I approached. White ibis and great blue herons poked about the shores or landed on the many short mangrove trees. A bald eagle swooped low, plucking a fish out of the water, clutching it in its talons. A manatee surfaced to take a breath of air. Dolphins splashed. This was a nature-lover's paradise, one enjoyed by people for thousands of years. Nothing could be better.

When I reached my island, it was sunset and I knew I didn't have much time to set up my tent, gather firewood, and cook dinner. I pulled my kayak onto the small sandy beach and spread out my tent. Then I started searching for firewood before it became dark. There was little wood around my camp—no surprise there, so I walked down one of many narrow trails that led into the island's interior. I soon found dead branches near the crumbling stone foundation of an old house, but it wasn't enough to keep a fire going for long. I searched in the shadows and pulled out a weathered flat piece of wood stuck in the ground, rounded at the top. Someone worked this at one time, I determined. Maybe it had been part of the house. Since it looked like old heart pine, I knew it would burn well.

**Wild island in the Mosquito Lagoon.**

Upon returning to my camp, I was surprised to see a man standing before my tent. He was small and frail looking, with long gray hair and a red beard. His eyes glared at me.

"You've disturbed me! What are you doing on my island?" he demanded. He eyed the slab of wood in my hand.

"Your island? This land is owned by the government, and I've got a permit to stay here. Where's yours?"

"Government be damned. I'm Red and this is my island!"

"No, it's not. You need to leave me alone. I'm tired and hungry and getting cold. I need to make a fire."

The old man snarled at me. Harmless old fool, I thought, but where did he come from, and how was he going to leave? I didn't see any other boat.

I broke up the wood and started a bright fire. The old man's eyes widened. He soon disappeared, so I heated up water for my freeze-dried lasagna and coffee. About the time the water began to boil, my guest returned. "I told you to get out!" he yelled.

"And I told YOU to get out. I have the permit, remember. Now leave me alone or I'll call the ranger." I popped open my cell phone and began dialing.

"I said out!" the man screamed.

He moved a wrinkled hand toward the fire, shaking it back and forth. Flames suddenly shot up eight feet into the air. I stepped back. My pots became completely blackened and most of the water spilled out.

"Now look what you've done," I said, becoming more irritated. "That was a cheap old gypsy trick. You threw some kind of powder into the fire."

I finished dialing the ranger and got a recording. "Hello," I said after the beep. "I have camping permit number eight and this lunatic named Red is trying to drive me away. I need someone to come out here and arrest him." I figured the threat of a night in jail would scare him. He didn't know I reached an answering machine.

Red turned beet red with anger. "You don't believe I can drive you from my island?" he cried. With that, he clapped his hands. Snakes began slithering from the brush and marsh grass. I reached for my kayak paddle and held it in front of me like a sword, but in the firelight, I soon determined these were nonvenomous species of snakes. I always had a keen fascination with snakes, especially as a boy. That sense of wonder returned to me.

"Wow, that's a rainbow snake!" I cried. "I haven't seen one of those in years. And over there is a mangrove snake, and there's a beautiful red rat snake. It just glistens in the light. It must have just shed. And there's a—"

"Arrrgh!" Red cried, obviously exasperated. "You need to leave my island!" He clapped his hands twice. The noise was like thunder, and the island itself rumbled. Suddenly, water began covering the island, gushing up through cracks in the mud. It rushed past my feet, then past my knees. I quickly found myself underwater, struggling for oxygen. A sudden image popped into my head—a grave, with a wooden marker. My grave? Then I noticed something familiar about the marker. It was a slab of weathered wood, like what I had used for firewood. It dawned on me—I had burned Red's grave marker!

Gasping for breath, I reached the surface and managed to grab my kayak and paddle before they floated away. I looked up to see Red hovering over the scene, bigger than life, and bathed in an eerie orange light. A wicked smile was splashed across his face. "Leave my island!" he cried.

"I . . . I'm sorry," I stammered, spitting out water. "I didn't know."

Red's eyes burned like fire. "Now!" he screamed. He moved his right arm in a wide arc and a huge wave erupted, sending me cascading away from shore. Somehow, I managed to crawl onto my kayak and seat myself, no easy task. I paddled away as fast as I could, a half-moon casting just enough light for me to see. I didn't look back until I covered at least a quarter of a mile, but when I did, I was shocked. My tent stood undisturbed beside a small fire; everything looked peaceful. Should I return? Then I felt my wet hair and clothes. I knew better. It was Red's Island, and he could have it.

## AUTHOR'S NOTES

I wrote this story soon after kayaking through part of Mosquito Lagoon. My job was to map a sea kayak trail around the entire state for the Florida Department of Environmental Protection. During my travels, I had often visited remote islands once inhabited by people, some of whom had been hermits. I found their stone foundations, old bottles, and other remnants of their existence. I often wondered what those early pioneers were like, and how they lived. Once, I found a remote cemetery on a now uninhabited coastal island and had the feeling that my presence had disturbed their eternal rest, and so the seeds for "Red's Island" were planted.

## MORE ABOUT THE INDIAN RIVER

The Indian River Lagoon is North America's most diverse estuary. Overlapping boundaries of tropical and subtropical climates have helped to create a natural system that supports 4,300 different kinds of plants and animals, about 50 of which are endangered or threatened. Sea turtles, manatees, dolphins, and a wide variety of bird life, from roseate spoonbills to bald eagles, can be seen in relative abundance, depending on the season.

Mosquito Lagoon, the setting for this story, is an inviting place of unspoiled islands and a labyrinth of tidal creeks that is sheltered from the Atlantic by Cape Canaveral and Merritt Island. This estuary is a vital nursery for fish, oysters, clams, shrimp, and other sea life and, not surprisingly, it's one of Florida's most famous fishing grounds.

The abundant life of the Indian River and Mosquito Lagoon estuaries have attracted people for thousands of years. Timucuan Indians annually migrated to these shores from inland areas to gather clams, oysters, and to catch fish. They left behind giant shell mounds, two of which can be seen today in Canaveral National Seashore—Seminole Rest and Turtle Mound. Other mounds were hauled away for fill material.

The adjacent Merritt Island National Wildlife Refuge, like the national seashore, was established as a buffer zone for nearby NASA activities. It covers 140,000 scenic acres of brackish estuaries, marshes, coastal dunes, scrub oaks, pine forests and flatwoods, and palm and oak hammocks.

Water degradation from human runoff is the main threat to the Indian River Lagoon, and while steps have been taken to control pollution, undeveloped protected areas such as Canaveral National Seashore are vital buffers for the Indian River.

## STORYTELLING TIPS

As you tell this tale, bear in mind that the character Red increases his power as he becomes more agitated. You can do the same with your voice. Begin Red's lines with a slight edge and increase the magnitude until Red's voice is filled with rage. Stand up and scream, "Leave my island!" and watch the wide-eyed expressions of your audience members. An optional prop, sure to get a stir from your audience, is to bring a nonvenomous snake in a pillowcase or basket and pull it out when Red conjures up snakes to scare away his intruder. Rubber snakes thrown out into the audience can yield fun results.

**Estimated Telling Time:** 10–11 minutes, depending on snakes

# · 10 ·

# Cypress Angel

$\mathscr{M}$y grandmother told me lots of stories when I was growing up, but the one I remember most was of two witches who lived in the swamp in cabins and battled each other during the pioneer days in rural North Florida. They had come from a remote area of Europe that was steeped in magic and mystery. One was considered a good witch who helped people with their problems, the other witch cast evil spells as she tried to selfishly help herself in any way possible.

When I first heard the story as a child, I conjured up images of the *Wizard of Oz*. The good witch would float in on a glowing bubble, dressed in white, wearing a crown, while the bad witch would be ugly, wearing a black robe and a pointed hat. But Grandma said these witches looked like most other folks, except they were powerful. When they started fighting, people could see sparks flying over the treetops and hear their screams. Everyone stayed clear. Finally, the bad witch just disappeared. No one saw her anymore, and her cabin sat abandoned and eventually lay in ruin, home to all kinds of swamp critters.

When someone finally got the courage to ask the good witch what happened, the woman smiled and said, "She became a tree. A cypress tree in a faraway swamp. And she'll stay that way for as long as that tree is standing. Cypress trees live longer than any other tree in these parts, sometimes more than a thousand years!" She winked and smiled again, but then added, more seriously, "But when that tree does fall, much destruction will follow."

Growing up, I never knew if this story was true or simply a lesson about not being selfish. If you're too selfish or mean, you'll turn into a cypress tree!

As an adult, I started kayaking. I loved to explore the back sloughs and swamps along the lower Apalachicola River in North Florida. The floodplain

**Canopied creek off the Apalachicola River.**

could be up to five miles wide in these parts, the widest of any Florida river, so there were lots of places to explore when the water was up.

One day I was kayaking with a friend exploring the many creeks and sloughs off Owl Creek along the lower river. We were paddling up one narrow slough beneath a beautiful canopy of cypress and tupelo gum trees when my friend suddenly announced, "I hear a voice."

"I don't hear anything," I said.

"It's a woman's voice, and it seems to be saying 'help me.'"

I cupped my hands around my ears. "I still don't hear it."

"You can't? That's hard to believe. It's a weak voice, but it's clear, and it's crying for help."

I felt a cold chill when she said that. The beautiful swamp suddenly took on an eerie quality. "I guess we'd better investigate then," I said half-hearted.

We paddled farther up the slough as it narrowed even more. It would have been impossible to bring anything but a kayak up this slough. That's one reason I enjoyed kayaking. It took you places motorboats couldn't reach, but I wasn't enjoying this trip. When the slough became very narrow and shallow, I suggested we turn around.

Cypress angel tree along creek near the Apalachicola River.

"No," said my friend. "Can't you hear it? The voice is even louder now!"

"Okay, but we can't make it much farther." We squeezed beneath two cypress trees and then a couple more before the creek widened again. Then we saw it—a lone mangled-looking cypress tree standing in a small pool of water, and it had a face and twisted arms! It seemed like a dark angel that was frozen in time.

"That's it!" said my friend, pointing to the tree. "That's where the voice is coming from. But, it's a tree, like a person in a tree, and she's crying."

I still couldn't hear the voice, but even though it was early summer, and it had been hot and humid, I felt cold and started shivering. "I believe you," I said, finally. "But we can't do anything to help. We have to go. I'll tell you the story later."

To block out the voice, my friend placed her hands over her ears and seemed ready to cry, but she took a deep breath, nodded, and picked up her paddle again. We turned around and left that place as quickly as possible, vowing never to return.

A couple of years later, in 2018, Hurricane Michael roared through the lower Apalachicola River area, a category 5 hurricane and the largest storm to hit the Florida Panhandle in recorded history. More than half the trees were reportedly toppled by huge winds. Was the cypress angel one of the trees that fell, breaking the spell? I wasn't going back to find out.

## AUTHOR'S NOTES

I came upon "cypress angel" a few years ago while kayaking the back sloughs along the lower Apalachicola River. This is truly a wild place where most of the land and waters are protected by either the State of Florida or the federal government. Unfortunately, the river has been deprived of water in recent decades by upstream sources in Georgia, so the sloughs are often drier than they should be. This affects trees, fish, wildlife, and the oysters and shrimp in Apalachicola Bay and the people who make a living harvesting them. The State of Florida and groups such as the Apalachicola Riverkeeper are fighting hard for increased water flows in the river.

In viewing the "cypress angel" from my kayak, I was amazed at this twisted cypress tree that resembled a human figure or "angel," and it had a face! There was no way of determining its age. This story provides one explanation as to how this tree came to look the way it does.

## STORYTELLING TIPS

As the story builds, ask the audience whether it is getting colder. And when you get to the story's climax, start to shiver uncontrollably and show the photo in this book of the real cypress angel.

**Estimated Telling Time:** 7–8 minutes

# Trapped along the Slave Canal

"My great-great grandfather ran cotton through here," said Hank, scanning the vine-covered opening of the Wacissa River's Slave Canal from the front of a canoe. "He had a plantation in northern Jefferson County. He needed a way to send his cotton to the Gulf of Mexico so it could be shipped to other states and countries. This was a natural stream that was deepened and widened, and it was used for only a few years in the 1850s until the railroad came. Then the place just went wild. Now the state owns the land around it, if you call it land. Mostly just worthless swamp. But I hear it's quite an adventure to get through it. That's why you brought me here, right Son."

Hank's son Jim nodded. Attending college in Tallahassee, he enjoyed exploring some of Florida's wildest places, but his dad mostly seemed to want to buy and sell land since he was a real estate broker. They had grown apart in recent years, so he thought this Slave Canal adventure might bring them closer together. It would be three more miles before they would take out where the canal emptied into the Aucilla River. Jim knew it could be slow going. Fallen trees often blocked the path, requiring lifting the canoe up and over them. Jim thought the team effort might bring them closer together.

While paddling beneath a canopy of cypress, gum, and bay trees, Hank looked around. He had to admit the place did have a certain primitive beauty. The bright green of sprouting leaves was striking, and the aroma of wax myrtle and willow bushes gave off a sweet, almost flower-like fragrance.

He saw flashes of yellow warblers moving through the trees and schools of silvery fish darting past in the water. Turtles plopped off logs and baby alligators ducked underwater.

They stopped at a wide tree-covered Indian mound for lunch. "This was built way before the canal," said Hank. "The Indians came through here with their dugout canoes."

**Georgia Ackerman paddles down the Wacissa Slave Canal.**

"Yeah, then the white men came with their dreams of a canal," said Jim, scoffing.

When they embarked again, they came upon a straight section of waterway where moss-covered boulders lined the shores. "Those boulders were put there by slaves, weren't they Pa?" asked Jim. "Our family's slaves. Right?"

"I guess you're right, Son. Great-great grandpa had lots of slaves."

"It must have been awful work, prying boulders out of the muck with shovels, pickaxes, and mules. It's nice for us gliding along in this canoe, but digging out this canal for weeks on end, sleeping out here in the swamps, that must have been awful with the bugs and heat."

Hank nodded, feeling quiet.

"And for what?" Jim continued. "To ship a few bales of cotton? And then the railroad came and made all this work for nothing."

"Great-great grandpa must have felt it was the best decision at the time."

"Yeah, but the men working here, they had no choice. No choice at all. It was wrong."

The two were quiet for awhile. They often disagreed about politics and different issues. "That happened a long time ago, Son. Maybe we should just let sleeping dogs lie."

Jim opened his mouth to say something and then stopped. He didn't want to argue.

**Boulders along the Wacissa Slave Canal were placed there by slaves in the 1850s who were working to deepen the waterway.**

They soon came to a large tree that had fallen across the stream. They had to stand on the log and pull the canoe over it. Around another bend, they came upon more moss-covered rocks piled along the shores and two fallen trees, one on top of the other. As they tried to steady themselves on the two logs while grabbing for the canoe to lift it over, the top tree shifted. Hank slipped, wedging his leg between the two trees. "Arrgh!" he cried. He couldn't budge the tree trunk or move his leg. "Do something!" he cried. "Do something!"

Jim reached for a canoe paddle and tried to pry the fallen tree away from his father's leg, but the paddle snapped in two. Then he tried finding a stout limb to pry it away, but the tree wouldn't budge. "I can't believe this," Hank cried, grimacing from pain. "We need some help. Call someone!"

Jim whipped out his cell phone. He pressed buttons and sighed. "No signal, Dad. It's too remote here."

"I can't believe it. You've got to do something. Go get help. Get some help!" Jim looked around the swampland in all directions. He wouldn't know which direction to take if he decided to go by foot for help, and it was muddy and wet. He doubted if he could make it out before dark, and what if he got lost, then what? It could be miles to a road. The only way out was by the canal. He would have to paddle the canoe out alone with the one good paddle that was left

"I'll go get help, Dad, but I hate to leave you alone."

"That's the only thing you can do, Son. Now get going!"

Jim paddled hard, but more fallen trees slowed him down, especially since he had to hoist the canoe over them by himself. For Hank, his leg was going numb. *How did I get into this mess?* he wondered. Everything happened so fast. He had never felt so alone and helpless.

Shadows grew as time passed, the only sounds being the gurgling stream, singing birds, and a few buzzing mosquitoes. Then the first owl started hooting and another answered. Cicadas began whirring in the treetops. But the next sound Hank heard was different and caused him to perk up. He thought he heard the clanking of a shovel, a shovel hitting rock. Help could be on its way. "Hello! Hello!" he shouted. "Over here."

No voice answered but he heard more shovels clanking on rocks. He peered into the growing darkness and only saw shadows rising from the darkening waters of the canal itself. He slowly made out figures, half human and half shadow. They moved closer to him, carrying shovels and pickaxes. And as they made a half circle around him, he could make out the dark faces of a dozen rugged men with lean bodies and soiled, torn clothes. They said nothing, just stared. Haunting stares. And Hank saw pain in those faces, desperation, and even pity. Pity for him who was trapped in this place.

"What do you want? What are you going to do to me?"

The figures looked at each other and nodded, moving closer. The men grunted "huh" in unison as they raised their tools high in the air.

"It wasn't me!" Hank cried. "It was great-great grandpa. Those were different times. All men are free now."

The grim expressions on the men remained unchanged. With another "huh," they suddenly dropped their tools and placed them under the tree that pinned Hank's leg. In sync, the ones with the shovels pushed down while those with pickaxes pulled. "Hah!" they called together. At first the fallen tree didn't move. "Hah!" they called again, louder, and some of the men groaned. Then the tree started rising, first a half inch, then an inch. Just enough for Hank to pull out his leg and free himself. "Ho!" the men cried and let the tree down and removed their tools. Hank breathed hard because the leg was stiff and throbbing, but he was no longer trapped. He was free. The men around him backed into a half circle again. Hank looked at each one of the figures with gratitude. "Thank you," he said. "Thank you. I will never forget what you did for me, and the work you did here." He thought he saw one of them smile a bit. They nodded to him before they backed away into the shadows and sunk back into the canal.

It was nightfall when Jim arrived by headlamp with a search and rescue team. "Dad, Dad, how did you get free?"

"The tree just shifted, that's all," said Hank. "It was a miracle. A true miracle."

Jim shook his head. "That's amazing. We couldn't budge it."

By headlamp, the crew helped Hank to an airboat about a half mile downstream. From there, there were no more fallen trees. They examined Hank's leg and determined it was not broken, just bruised and stiff. On the way home he told Jim, "We need to find some way to honor those men who built that canal. Their work must not be forgotten. People need to know the whole story of the Wacissa River Slave Canal." Jim looked at him and nodded in agreement, the first time they had agreed on something like this in a long while.

## AUTHOR'S NOTES

The Wacissa River Slave Canal, dug by slaves through a thick swamp forest in the 1850s, is one of North Florida's wildest streams. I have kayaked and

**The beauty of the wild Wacissa Slave Canal.**

canoed through the canal many times and it can be difficult to find and challenging to navigate due to fallen trees, but its scenic beauty is unsurpassed. Canoes or kayaks and a guide are recommended.

Slaves were forced to build the canal in wet, humid conditions, fighting bugs and malaria, and contending with all sorts of misery and discomfort. Nature has erased signs of that toil except for piles of rocks along some stretches.

A few years ago, the Florida Fish and Wildlife Conservation Commission, as part of a statewide effort toward racial sensitivity regarding geographic names, proposed renaming the waterway "Cotton Run Canal." The Jefferson County Commission and several individuals familiar with the canal, including African American leaders, opposed the name change. In January 2006, the U.S. Board on Geographic Names voted to keep the original name, citing a lack of local support for the name change. The Slave Canal remains the official name, serving to remind visitors of the men who built it.

The idea for this story came when I helped to guide a descendent of a local plantation owner on a kayak trip down the wild waterway.

## STORYTELLING TIPS

When Hank is trapped, make sure to inflect a tone of panic in your voice and a tone of real fear when the figures appear.

**Estimated Telling Time:** 8–9 minutes

# • *12* •

# The Golden Bear

*O*ld Man Parker could barely speak. He was on his deathbed, and he had asked for me. I was twelve-years-old at the time and had been delivering the Parker's newspaper for more than a year. Mr. Parker couldn't read due to a childhood case of the mumps that had left him blind, so his wife read the paper to him. He enjoyed my monthly visits to collect money for the paper.

Mr. Parker often told me stories of his childhood around Charlotte Harbor before he lost his sight: tromping through woods and swamps and sailing to islands. He also told stories that had been passed down to him by his grandparents of early Indians, Spaniards, Florida cowboys, and fishermen. Being blind at a young age, he spent more time around the adults than his brothers, sisters, and cousins, and he became a good listener. By the time he was an adult, he had become a keeper of the family stories.

Mr. Parker's voice was often strong and lively when he spoke. He described things in a colorful way. I didn't need a television set to see the things he talked about. But lying in bed like that, Mr. Parker could only whisper.

"Come closer, Doug," he rasped when he heard me enter the room. He had learned to tell people apart by the sounds they made when they walked, and if they were an adult or child by the way the wood floor creaked. I hesitated. Death was the greatest mystery of all. It could frighten both young and old, and Mr. Parker would soon explore that mystery as would all of us one day. I slowly slid into the chair beside the bed, glad Mr. Parker couldn't see my troubled face.

"Doug," he began weakly, "I'm sorry you have to see me this way. I'm about to meet my maker. That part I'm looking forward to, but I thought I would have more time." He paused, and I sensed a sadness come over him. "I have told you many of my stories," he continued, "but not all. Some will die with me, and I suppose a certain number die with each generation, to make room for those that follow. There is one, however, that you should hear. I have thought about it every day of my life. Do you have time for me to tell it?"

"Why yes, Mr. Parker," I said. "I have time. My parents said I could stay late tonight."

"Good. I know you probably have to study for school, but this is my one request. Since I have no children who are living—my boy Robbie was lost in the war, you know—you are the one to pass this on to because you have a good heart."

"Why sure," I said. "I'm listening."

"Well, it begins like this. There was this old Calusa chief who lived on Pine Island along Charlotte Harbor. We no longer know his name, but we know something about his people. The Calusas were once a powerful tribe— they ruled most of South Florida and developed a sophisticated civilization. They were known as the Fierce People. Even the early Spaniards were afraid of them. This chief was one of the last of his people, however. Most Calusas had died of diseases brought by the Europeans. Entire villages had been wiped out. This troubled the chief greatly. His people were disappearing before his eyes. They were becoming extinct like some animals."

Mr. Parker took a labored breath and continued. "Before the chief passed onto the spirit world, he had one important task to do. He had been entrusted with a valuable object that had been hidden from the white people, one that had been passed down in his family for several generations. It had been a gift from people across the Gulf of Mexico who had sometimes visited Florida by way of huge dugout canoes rigged with sails. The gift was a statue of a bear about a foot high that was so heavy it took both arms to lift. It was made of pure gold. It was given to the chief's family because they were members of the bear clan. The black bear was their special animal.

"To the Indians, gold was a pretty metal, so soft that it could easily be molded. But to the white people, gold was often placed above all else. It could make men crazy with greed. The chief wisely kept the golden bear hidden, that is, until it looked as though his people would disappear.

"He instructed the few remaining members of his clan to follow him deep into a swamp. At first, they canoed along a canal his people had dug long before—the Calusas built a network of canals throughout South Florida—then they waded to a small rise that was really a shell mound built by their ancestors. If you climbed a tree, you could see that the mound was shaped like a bear. It was here, in the head of the bear mound, where they buried the golden bear."

"But how do you know the story if this was all so secret?" I interrupted.

Mr. Parker chuckled weakly. "I knew you'd ask that question, Doug. You are inquisitive. You're wondering if I might be making this up, to pull your leg one last time. But I'll tell you why I'm not." He paused for a moment and cocked his head toward the door, listening, then continued. "You see, my great-great grandmother was the chief's granddaughter. She married a trader after most of her people died off. She knew about the buried statue and passed the story onto a chosen child or grandchild. Eventually, the story was passed down to me."

"So this golden bear is just sitting there in that mound?" I asked.

Mr. Parker smiled. "I suppose it is. I've always wanted to look for it, just to hold it, but I was blind." He sighed. "I didn't trust anyone else enough to find it for me." His voice became weaker and I had to lean over, putting my ear to his mouth. "Maybe you can find it one day, Doug. Hold it for me. Think of the Calusa. Promise me you will someday."

I nodded, feeling dry-mouthed, then remembered Mr. Parker could not see me. "I promise," I muttered.

"Remember," he continued, barely audible, "that statue was doctored with bear medicine. First, you'll need to—."

Mr. Parker closed his eyes then and gave a long sigh. He didn't breathe any air back in.

Six years later, I had my own car and a bit of freedom to venture off on my own. Not forgetting my promise, I purchased aerial photos from the Department of Transportation and looked through several archaeology books at the state library in Tallahassee about the Charlotte Harbor area. There were numerous shell mounds left by the Calusa, and some modern-day people even lived on top of the tallest mounds because they were high ground, keeping them above floodwaters caused by storms and hurricanes, but one spot in particular drew my interest—a small mound in a mangrove swamp that vaguely resembled a bear. You had to use a bit of imagination to see the shape—maybe you had to know the story—but I felt sure it was the bear mound. That part of Mr. Parker's story appeared to be true. Was the golden bear true as well? I told my parents I was going camping—not an unusual thing for me—and I set off toward South Florida with a canoe strapped atop my old Volkswagen.

After driving all day, I stayed at a small motor court near Punta Gorda. I had trouble falling asleep. Every time I closed my eyes, I saw black bears standing on their hind legs, alert, as if watching me from the edge of a forest. They weren't aggressive, just watching.

At first light, I pulled out my Charlotte County map and followed several side roads. At a dead end along Pine Island, I unstrapped the canoe and slid it into a canal that had originally been dug by Calusa Indians centuries before. I had a shovel and a borrowed metal detector wrapped in a tarp. I placed them in the bow of the boat, along with some food and water. Following a path I had marked on an aerial photo, I paddled along a network of overgrown canals through a thick mangrove swamp. Two hours later, I pulled up to a small clearing. I slung the shovel and metal detector over my shoulder and began sloshing through mud.

The chest-high mound wasn't obvious at first, being overgrown with shrubs and trees. It was not nearly as impressive as taller mounds I had seen, but I was convinced it was an Indian shell mound because of the cedar trees. Cedars often thrive in the calcium-rich soil created by discarded shells. My heart began to pound. I was eager to begin my search, but also hesitant. What was Mr. Parker trying to tell me before he died, something about bear medicine?

I felt funny stepping onto the mound, like I was entering unknown territory. I had the strange sensation I was being watched or followed. Trying to shrug it off, I looked for the "head" of the mound and slowly circled. I flicked on the metal detector and scanned close to the ground. Without this instrument I could be digging for days, and I didn't want to disturb any of the other artifacts that may have been buried in the mound. I had made a promise to Mr. Parker to only dig up the golden bear and look at it.

**Amateur archaeologist Dr. Leslie Weedon standing near a large Indian mound in southwest Florida in the early 1900s. Photo courtesy of the Florida Archives.**

"Here," a voice seemed to whisper in my ear. "Dig here." I turned to see the source of the voice, but somehow knew I wouldn't see anyone. I suspected it was Mr. Parker, guiding from the spirit world. I shivered. I stopped and scanned the ground thoroughly with the detector. The normally slow and steady beep quickened. Something more than discarded shells was underground.

"Here we go," I announced to no one in particular, and began digging. The shells made it difficult; I scraped more than dug. If there was a golden bear below, I didn't want to dent it with the shovel blade. Mosquitoes whined and the sun grew hot, but I didn't stop. Not then. Not until I had dug almost knee deep and scraped away a layer of oyster shells to reveal a shiny glint of gold. I couldn't believe it. I knelt, pushed away some dirt, and touched the head of the golden bear. It was like feeling the pulse of a lost people. I dug the hole wider and loosened shells around the statue. Then, very carefully, I placed both hands around it and pulled. It was extremely heavy. My breath was labored as I laid the statue outside the hole and wiped away centuries of accumulated dirt.

Staring up at me was a bear statue of pure gold, untarnished, with eyes of green jade. It was the most magnificent object I had ever seen, something you might view behind glass in the Smithsonian or in a King Tut exhibit, not in a South Florida swamp. This was an Indiana Jones adventure come true. Many thoughts began racing through my mind. If I brought the bear to the outside world, my photo would be splashed across every newspaper in the country, that is, if I didn't get arrested first for illegally digging artifacts. And what about the bear's value? All that gold would surely be worth millions. I might never have to work or go to school again.

Deciding to leave, I lifted the bear and turned. A sudden strangeness came over me. My thinking was cloudy, as if I could no longer formulate words in my head. *What was going on?* I wondered. Feeling pulled to the earth, I dropped to my knees. That's when I looked at my arms. They were becoming furry. I was too young to grow so many body hairs. Then it hit me—the bear medicine! I was becoming a bear! I had to act quickly. Cradling the heavy bear statue in one arm, I grunted and crawled over to the hole I had dug and carefully placed the golden bear exactly as I found it. Then I covered it and packed the ground. "There, you'll be safe now," I said, feeling better. "Mr. Parker, you were right. There is a golden bear, and he needs to stay right here, among the Calusa."

Leaving the mound that day, I felt light and happy, as if I had passed—barely—some sort of test. Paddling down the canals to my car, I felt many eyes upon me—Calusa eyes, Mr. Parker's eyes, and maybe that of a black bear or two. But after I returned home, many people wondered how I could have grown a full beard—and chest hairs where there were none before—in only two days. Plus, I had a sudden craving for raw acorns. I'd eat them shells and all, and thought they were mighty tasty.

## AUTHOR'S NOTES

I've told many versions of the golden bear story to summer camp kids over the years. Once, I buried a brass bear, covered the spot with leaves, and shared a story like this one. After telling the tale, students in my group begged to search for the golden bear. When I finally relented, I instructed them in the fine art of archaeological digging and we set off on the quest. I pointed to landmarks in the story that marked the spot—a rock and a large tree. The young people went crazy when they found the "golden bear." After their screaming subsided, I made the excuse that we would have to treat it like a valuable artifact and send it to the Smithsonian Institute in Washington, DC, for verification; I had the students help me fill out a legal-looking form. A few days later, I received calls from curious parents asking if the Smithsonian had responded. They said their children were driving them crazy with stories and questions about the golden bear, so I had to fess up.

I still have the fake golden bear. It sits on a shelf near my desk. I smile when I examine the indentation on its back from where an overzealous student struck it with a shovel during its excavation.

## MORE ABOUT THE CALUSA

In 1896, Marco Island, then called Key Marco, yielded some of the most astounding American Indian artifacts ever found in Florida. Digging in the island's mangrove muck, Frank Hamilton Cushing and his Smithsonian expedition crew uncovered an incredible array of objects from the Calusa people— exquisitely carved and painted wood animal heads, masks, clubs, bowls, and atlatls (spear-throwing devices). They also found nets, fishhooks, cord, ropes, floats, and shell jewelry. Cushing later wrote of these early craftsmen, "their art is not only an art of the sea, but is an art of shells and teeth, an art for which the sea supplied nearly all the working parts of tools, the land only some of the materials worked upon."

Some of the Calusa's ingenious tools included a saber made from shark teeth, and an axe blade made from a large sharpened conch shell.

With shell tools, the Calusa dug canals in their Southwest Florida environment to link important waterways. Some were eight feet deep, thirty feet wide, and up to fourteen miles long. In order to move more safely on open water, two dugout canoes were sometimes joined to make a catamaran with decks covered with awnings and matting. They used nets and even artificial lures to catch fish. Refusing to be farmers, the sea was their chief source of bounty. They supplemented catches of fish and shellfish with wild plant foods such as saw palmetto berries, cocoplum, papaya, hogplum, acorns, prickly pears, grapes, seagrapes, mastic, and red and black mangroves. They also hunted land animals such as deer.

With the sea providing an ample food supply, the Calusa evolved into a powerful society supported by an elite military. Their numbers may have reached one hundred thousand. They struck fear into neighboring tribes, exacting gifts of tribute in return for relative peace. They were accomplished seamen, sometimes sailing to Cuba and up and down the west coast of Florida. They are known to have attacked Spanish ships that were anchored close to shore, and they salvaged Spanish shipwrecks. Their arrows, often tipped with fish bone or shark's teeth, could penetrate Spanish armor at close range.

Early Spanish accounts help to bring Calusa culture to life. During an expedition to rescue shipwrecked Spanish sailors, Pedro Menendez de Aviles

**Calusa Indian display at the Florida Museum of Natural History in Gainesville.**

described entering the Calusa town of Carlos, located near present-day Fort Myers. He said it contained about four thousand men and women with a palm-thatched chief's house that could comfortably hold about half that number. Upon their arrival, about five hundred girls between the ages of ten and fifteen sang a song while other Indians whirled and danced.

One important Calusa town was at Pineland, occupied for more than 1,500 years on the northwestern shore of Pine Island along Charlotte Harbor, the setting for this story. Remains of an ancient canal are evident along with huge shell mounds.

Disease killed the majority of Calusa, and many survivors fell prey to enemy tribes in the 1700s. A handful of Calusa Indians fled to Cuba in 1763 when the British took control of Florida from Spain.

## STORYTELLING TIPS

In relaying Mr. Parker's lines as he tells the tale of the golden bear, gradually speak softer as he becomes weaker and weaker. Just before he dies, lower your voice to a near whisper. Your audience should be craning their necks to hear you. Then you can return to your normal voice as you continue the story.

When digging into the mound, you can pantomime digging movements and then stop with a look of wonder on your face as you see the first glint of gold. A bit of melodrama always helps, especially when the bear spell takes hold and you fall to the ground holding the golden bear. People, even adults, will sometimes believe your story because they want to believe, and a good storyteller always maintains the truth and accuracy of each story—to a point. Winks and the crossing of fingers are optional.

You can always deviate from this story and bury a brass bear at a key location (not an actual archaeological site) as I once did. Some young person in your audience will inevitably pipe up and say, "Let's go find it!" The more you try to discourage, the more insistent they will become, and so you reluctantly point out locations of digging tools and help them find the exact spot, cautioning your diggers to use extreme caution, and warning them of the bear spell.

**Estimated Telling Time:** 14–15 minutes

# • *13* •

# The Portal

*I*t was a complete surprise. Ned Raines had been hunting deer deep in the Chassahowitzka Swamp just north of Weeki Wachi when he stumbled upon a wild spring, clear and blue, about the size of a baseball diamond. The outflow formed a small stream that Ned assumed snaked its way to the Gulf of Mexico, about five miles distant.

Since it was fall, Ned admired how russet gold cypress needles reflected on the spring's surface along with orange and red leaves of gum and swamp maple. Swamplands were the best places to appreciate fall in Central and North Florida. The wild spring was a fitting mirror.

Ned stepped closer to the spring, working his way around a jumble of cypress knees. Hugging the bank, he rested his gun against a cypress trunk, crouched down, and leaned over. He expected to peer into the spring's cavernous depths but jumped back in shock. Staring up at him, as if standing on dry land, was a bare-chested dark-skinned man with long black hair, a, American Indian. What should he do? Ned's first impulse was to leave, get away from this mysterious place, but curiosity got the best of him. He grabbed his gun, somehow feeling more secure with the smooth stock hooked in his arm and leaned over again. What he saw was a scene playing out before him, as if the spring had become a movie screen.

He saw the American Indian man just inside the mouth of a cave that had a pool of clear water inside. *Could it be the same place thousands of years before when the water table was much lower?* Ned wondered. Fascinated, he watched the man, who wore only a loincloth, begin filling some sort of skin bag with water. Just then, the man turned sharply and stepped back in horror when he was confronted with a huge tan beast with two long curving teeth—a saber-toothed cat! Ned watched, wide-eyed, as the American Indian slowly moved

Wild spring in the swamps of the Chassahowitzka Wildlife Management Area near Weeki Wachee.

toward his slender cane spear and spear thrower while the beast crouched, ready to pounce. Ned knew the man had little chance against such an animal, especially since his spear was several feet away. One swipe or bite and it would be over.

Ned was so caught up in the scene he no longer felt like an observer. It was as if he were there. Instinctively, he brought the rifle to his shoulder. When the cat leapt, Ned pulled the trigger. The shot rang out and water seemed to erupt. The blast echoed through the swamp, and then all was quiet. Not even birds sang. Looking down after the water smoothed, Ned saw nothing except for an underwater cave and branches and trees that had fallen into the wild spring. *Was it all a dream?* he wondered. He waited and watched. Nothing. Finally, as sunlight slanted through the trees, he turned to leave.

Ned didn't see the water moccasin sunning lazily by the water's edge. When he stepped on its tail, the startled snake reared back in surprise, cottonmouth agape and fangs exposed. Ned knew he would be too slow to avoid the lightning quick strike. A whooshing sound suddenly came from the spring. A stone-tipped spear pierced the snake's flared neck, pinning the writhing creature to a cypress trunk. Ned noticed ripples spreading out from a spot near his feet. He nodded his thanks and left the wild spring, vowing never to return.

★ ★ ★

Argus had heard of a wild spring in the Chassahowitzka Swamp that had healing and magical properties. Florida had a history of healing waters that drew people with numerous kinds of physical ailments. Resorts were built around these springs, which were slightly sulfuric—smelling like a lost Easter egg—and easily accessible along a rail line or river. Very few were in the middle of a swamp.

Argus was not searching for the spring because he had a physical ailment, even though his joints ached from bursitis. He came because of a broken heart. He had once been a sponge fisherman hailing from Tarpon Springs, back when the port bustled with fishermen and docks were loaded high with fresh-caught sponges. Argus had had a boat, a small crew, and a beautiful wife, Daphne. They were living a fantasy—the American Dream. Then a hurricane hit while they were on the water. He lost a crewman, and he lost Daphne. A massive red tide bloom struck a year later, and the sponge industry never recovered, and neither did Argus.

The journey to the spring was difficult for the sad old man, but when he finally reached the swampy shore, he was filled with youthful hope. He didn't know what to expect when he gazed into the deep-blue depths. At first, he saw nothing—only submerged logs and a cave opening. Then the spring clouded over and a scene began to play out before him. Argus saw himself as

**A hiker searches for springs in the swamps of the Chassahowitzka Wildlife Management Area.**

a young man, full of vigor and life, and he saw Daphne and the sponge boat. The crew was fitting him with a diving bell and then lowering him into the water while feeding him an air line. He glimpsed the often-surreal world of the ocean floor—corals, sponges, and sea fans of all shapes and colors along with an array of fish and other marine creatures. What a life! He'd gather sponges, the crew would clean them, and when they returned to Tarpon Springs after days or weeks, eager buyers paid top dollar. It was as good a living as he could have ever dreamed. He would give anything to go back. And when Argus touched the cold spring water, that's exactly what he did.

★ ★ ★

"You'll have to be the man of the house now," said Lois, Chad's mother, soon after his father suddenly died of heart failure. Chad felt an uncomfortable heaviness come over him. He didn't feel much like a man, not at age eleven with his skinny body and buckteeth. Kids at school called him "Bean Pole" or "Buck."

Chad was lonely without his father, especially on Saturdays. Living near Weeki Wachi, he and his father used to explore the Chassahowitzka swamp forest on their "Saturday adventures." On one occasion, they found the vine-covered foundations of Centralia, a former logging town of more than 1,500

**The ruins of the logging town of Centralia from the early 1900s in the Chassahowitzka Wildlife Management Area.**

people. The town had been abandoned in the 1920s after all the large cypress and pines had been cut.

On another outing they stumbled upon a wild spring in the middle of the swamp. That had been a special day with his dad. The April air seemed to tingle as colorful yellow and black warblers flew past. They saw deer nimbly move through the swamp, and the highlight was when they glimpsed a black bear. His father explained that only about twenty bears lived in the area, possibly the smallest known bear population in North America. They were isolated and nearly surrounded by development and busy highways. Many were killed trying to cross roads. Since that outing Chad had developed a keen interest in the plight of the Chassahowitzka bears.

Remembering the wild spring, Chad decided to visit it again and think about his new and unexpected role as man of the family. His father had once said that when seeking direction, he should spend time alone in the woods, and the answer might come. When Saturday arrived, Chad awoke early, left a note for his mother, and rode his mountain bike as far as he could down unpaved roads. Then he began hiking and wading. His father had taught him how to use a compass and he frequently paused to check his bearings. Remembering the previous outing, he walked almost straight to the spring. There was no trail.

To Chad, the wild spring was a hidden jewel, one that few people visited. Sunlight slanted through the depths like facets of a blue-tinted sapphire. Along the water's edge, he leaned over and peered into the cavernous depths. When he did, he momentarily glimpsed a familiar reflection next to his—that of his father. Chad was not afraid. It made him feel tingly. This was a magical spot.

Chad sat quietly and ran his fingers through the cool water. He watched butterflies catch sunlight with their colorful wings. He breathed deep. The peace he felt was welcoming. He returned his gaze to the spring's depths and was surprised to see it cloud over. A scene began forming of a strapping young man, handsome and confident-looking, directing workers in building some sort of wide tunnel beneath a highway. In an instant, Chad knew everything about the project—it was a wildlife underpass especially geared toward the endangered Chassahowitzka bears. A fence on both sides of the road would direct wildlife toward the underpass and beneath the busy highway. The Chassahowitzka bears and other animals could then safely travel to other large undeveloped land areas, such as the Withlacoochee State Forest. And the young man? Chad realized it was his future self.

As the scene slowly disappeared, a swallowtail kite swooped low, skimmed the spring's surface with its beak to gulp fresh water, and soared again over the treetops. Chad watched until the scissor-tailed bird flew out of sight. He followed suit by scooping up a mouthful of water, savoring the cool trickle down his throat. He felt lighter somehow, hopeful. The dark days of mourning seemed distant. He was a boy becoming a man, and he knew his father would never completely leave him in his quest to help the Chassahowitzka black bears.

## AUTHOR'S NOTES

A visit to a wild spring in the Chassahowitzka Wildlife Management Area near Weeki Wachi inspired this story. To reach the spring involved careful maneuvering through a thick cypress swamp. Gazing into the spring's clear blue depths, it was easy to imagine the early native people and animals that once utilized these springs. Even mastodons and saber-toothed cats likely drank from the pure waters. When visiting Florida's springs, I've often wondered, "If only the waters could talk, the tales they could tell."

## MORE ABOUT FLORIDA'S SPRINGS

Having 320 known springs, Florida may have the highest concentration in the world, discharging nearly eight billion gallons a day. Some are huge, cavernous affairs—known as first-magnitude springs—while others are small trickles. Springs are found in rivers, lakes, the Gulf of Mexico, and Atlantic Ocean. Some rivers, such as the Wakulla, Ichetucknee, and Rainbow, receive most of their base flow from springs, while the wide Suwannee River receives about half of its flow from springs. Springs are portals, or windows, into the vast underground reservoir known as the Floridan aquifer, located in the northern half of the state.

Florida's abundance of springs is due to the porous limestone and dolomite that underlies most of the state. A weak carbonic acid, formed by rainwater and decaying vegetation seeping into the ground, slowly dissolves the underlying rocks, creating cracks, caverns, and cavities. Since groundwater is constantly under pressure from incoming surface water, water is pushed through this "rock sponge" base and out through natural surface openings, known as springs. Thus, springs serve as relief valves for a highly pressurized system.

Springs support a diversity of life, ranging from American eels to unique crayfish. Some animals deep inside underwater caves never see the light of day. The nearly constant temperature of springs often provides a winter refuge for Florida's manatees.

Florida springs have also supported and fascinated people. Springs explorer Doug Stamm writes in his book *The Springs of Florida*: "Ancient cultures that first ventured into Florida long ago found primitive security in the plentiful food and campsites spring areas provided. In the mysteries of these upwelling waters their religions and legends were founded. Though little evidence remains of these early inhabitants, relics of their stone-age cultures and fossilized bones of their prey are found underwater among spring sands."

In more recent years, human activity has been detrimental to the water quality of many Florida springs. Urban runoff, wastewater spray fields, septic tanks, fertilizers, agricultural runoff, vehicle fluids, and other pollution sources often seep into the groundwater and show up in springs. Exotic weeds in some springs, boosted by high nitrogen concentrations in the water, can nearly cover spring openings and clog spring runs. "Springs die a slow death of a thousand wounds," said Jim Stevenson, former chairman of the Florida Springs Task Force. Sadly, pollution in springs directly correlates with population growth.

Solutions are readily available: reuse of reclaimed water on golf courses and rights of way; better treatment and filtration of pollution; regular maintenance of septic tanks or the use of advanced septic systems; more sensitivity in the use of fertilizers and pesticides; innovative alternatives to sprayfields such as artificial wetlands; and protecting a spring's recharge basin from intense development. To successfully clean up and protect our springs depends on how serious we are about our stewardship responsibilities.

Despite the threats and challenges, a visit to a Florida spring has a way of stretching out time and giving one perspective. Author Al Burt writes, "Whatever the distractions and distortions around them—however strip-zoned and ugly the road there might be, and however concreted and constrained those once sandy banks might have become—springs still can deliver a living piece of Florida that performs much the same way it did during our childhood, and even before that.

"Springs add a melody to the land."

## STORYTELLING TIPS

When telling these tales of the magical spring, keep looking down as if gazing with wonder into a deep pool of clear water. This will help create an air of mystery for your listeners. You can even use a blue or clear globe to represent the spring in your storytelling, viewing it like a crystal ball. When Ned Raines shoots his gun into the water, liven up your audience by spraying them with water from a spray bottle.

As a follow-up to the story about the endangered Chassahowitzka black bears, you can present more information about Florida's black bears and ways we can live more compatibly with these large mammals. Contact the Florida Fish and Wildlife Conservation Commission or join the Defenders of Wildlife's Habitat for Bears campaign.

**Estimated Telling Time:** 11–12 minutes

# · *14* ·

# Nogoshomi

$\mathcal{R}$obert thought it was the perfect vacation—canoeing for three days with his ten-year-old daughter, Amanda, down the Withlacoochee River. They were skirting an area known as The Cove—a maze of lakes, islands, and swamps bordered on three sides by the river. Seminole Indians once hid here and successfully fought off several large armies during the Second Seminole War. Being a historian, Robert was teaching Amanda about Florida's past by visiting places where events occurred. On the second night, he carefully selected a campsite on a high sandy bank shaded by live oak trees and surrounded by thick palmettos.

"This is great," said Robert to Amanda, standing on the bank. "We are near where Osceola and hundreds of Seminoles fought large armies on two different occasions, forcing them to retreat. You can see why. From here, you can spot anyone coming, and pick off soldiers trying to cross the river. The Seminoles were safe on this side of the river for a long time, even though thousands of soldiers were after them."

Amanda nodded. Being on the river with her father helped her visualize historic events that took place better than just reading about them in a book. "When did all this happen?"

"In the 1830s."

"What happened to the Seminoles?" She didn't remember seeing any Indians along the river, only some fishermen.

"During the war, they finally left this place when armies came after them from different directions. They eventually retreated into the Everglades where they fought for several more years. Most were eventually killed or sent to Oklahoma, though some of their descendants still live in the Everglades."

"Oh." Amanda felt disappointed. She wanted to meet some Seminoles. "Can we see where they used to live, their old villages?"

91

**Early morning scene on the Withlacoochee River.**

"Those are long gone, honey. Not much lasts for very long in Florida. The jungle just takes over."

Father and daughter decided to cook spaghetti for dinner. Amanda volunteered to filter river water in order to boil the noodles. She walked to the shore and leaned over to pump water into the pot. Just then, she heard a loud booming sound and a huge splash, as if someone had thrown a giant boulder into the river. She then saw several large brown furry creatures running through the brush on the opposite shore. They were larger than raccoons but smaller than bears. Otherwise, she could not make out other features.

Amanda rushed up the embankment to tell her father. Robert had heard the noise and smiled. "Probably just beavers," he said.

"But they were bigger than that. And what could have made that big noise and splash?"

"Maybe they were exceptionally large beavers, and that splash was one of their tails hitting the water." Robert noticed Amanda's frown, and so he offered, "Then again, maybe they were something else."

"Like what?"

"Well, I was down in the Everglades awhile back doing some research and this old Seminole woman told me about some supernatural creatures that travel between worlds. She said they were bear-like creatures called the nogoshomi."

Amanda cocked her head and smiled. "Uh, I don't think so."

Robert smiled too. "Yeah, I had the feeling she was just pulling my leg. Let's go down and take a look."

They slowly approached the shore, but all was quiet except for the trickling sounds of a flowing river. "Oh well, they must have left," said Robert as he bent down to finish filling the cook pot with water. Amanda squinted her eyes. *What were they?* She wondered.

After dinner, Robert announced he was going down to the river to wash dishes. "Who knows, maybe our furry friends are back, and I'll get to see them," he said.

Amanda thought for a moment, then announced, "No, I'll go. I'm not afraid."

"Are you sure, honey? I'll go with you."

"No, I'll be okay." Amanda wasn't so sure, but she wanted to prove she was brave.

"I'll watch from up there then," said Robert.

Amanda nervously walked down the slope toward the river in the growing darkness. She began filling the spaghetti pot when she heard the booming sound and witnessed the same type of huge splash as before. Then she saw the brown furry creatures running through the brush, only this time they were on her side of the river. Robert witnessed everything and stood up. "You okay, Amanda?" he yelled.

"Dad, come down here."

As her father fumbled for a flashlight, Amanda noticed that the furry creatures had stopped running and were moving toward her. They were about three feet tall, brown and furry, but other details were hazy. She began to back away from the river when something grabbed her ankle and pulled her into the water. "Daddy!" she cried.

Robert raced down the slope and dove in after Amanda. He reached for her arm just as she was being pulled under. "Amanda! Amanda!" he screamed. He dove under and tried to find her in the dark water, feeling with his hands. Nothing. He dove repeatedly, fighting the strong current, but couldn't find her. Finally, exhausted, he swam to shore and shone the flashlight across the river. Nothing. Frantic, he ran up and down the bank calling her name. After several minutes he stopped, dropped down into the sand, and buried his face in his hands, weeping. "Amanda," he cried. "I've lost Amanda."

Robert felt a cold hand touch his shoulder. He jumped. He looked up to see Amanda, pale and wet. "Amanda!" he cried out in relief. "Are you alright?" He held her to make sure she wasn't a ghost. She felt real, but distant.

"Daddy, how long have I been gone?"

"What do you mean?"

"How long have I been gone?"

It seemed an unusual question for someone who had almost drowned. "Oh, about fifteen minutes," he responded. "What happened?"

"I feel like I've been gone a long, long time," she said. "It's another world down there."

"What world? What dragged you under?"

"I can't say. I promised not to say. That's the only way they let me come back."

"Who are they?"

Amanda pursed her lips, shaking her head.

"Okay, okay, you don't have to talk about it. I'm just glad you are safe." He hugged her again and led her away from the water, back to camp. He was surprised at her apparent lack of fear. She only seemed bewildered, and somehow more grown up.

While Amanda changed into dry clothes, Robert heated up water on a camp stove for hot chocolate. So strange, he thought. So very strange. Amanda returned and sat quietly on a log next to him. She still seemed miles away. "I've been gone for a long time," she said, "to another world. They taught me things, showed me things, and they said we must change. They've been watching us for a long time."

"Us? You mean you and me?"

"No, people. All people. We must stop polluting or both of our worlds will die."

"Wow. They said that?"

Amanda nodded. "They are hiding like the Seminoles once did. They are running out of places to go, places without a lot of people, places that are clean."

Robert couldn't resist asking the question again: "But who are they?"

"I can't tell you," she said. "I can't tell anyone."

And she never did.


## AUTHOR'S NOTES

This story was inspired by a solo camping trip along a wild river where I encountered mysterious water beings like the ones described in the story. Spooked, I promptly packed my gear and exited by flashlight. Relaying the story to a Seminole elder several years later, she said I had encountered the no-goshomi, supernatural creatures. The word for bear in the Muscogee language is *nogoshi*, so I surmised that "nogoshomi" meant bear-like creatures. American Indians describe many different types of supernatural creatures, so before you discount them as simply myths or tall tales, bear in mind that native people have lived in this land for many thousands of years longer than more recent arrivals from Europe and other lands, so they've had far longer to ponder the many mysteries that lie beneath the waters and in wild places.

## MORE ABOUT THE SECOND SEMINOLE WAR

Most historians contend that the Second Seminole War was more about slavery than about land. Slaves were escaping into Florida by the droves, mostly from Alabama and Georgia. And while the Seminoles also owned slaves, their form of slavery was generally far different than that of settlers or other southeastern tribes. As author Charles Hudson explains in his book *Southeastern Indians*: "Their slaves lived in comparative freedom, their only obligation being to pay their masters a portion of their corn, livestock, or animal skins each year. Some of the blacks among the Seminoles were freedmen who enjoyed the same rights as Indians and had the same voice in community affairs."

When Andrew Jackson, the Seminoles' nemesis in the First Seminole War, was elected president in 1828, he pushed the Indian Removal Act through Congress that ordered the relocation of every southeastern American Indian tribe to present-day Oklahoma. As a result, the Treaty of Paynes Landing was put forth to the Seminoles in 1832. It spelled out their removal within thirty-six months. A few chiefs signed and some Indians made the move, but leaders such as Osceola vowed to fight "till the last drop of Seminole blood has moistened the dust of his hunting ground." His resistance prompted a brief imprisonment by the Indian agent Wiley Thompson, an act that only fueled Osceola's anger.

In December 1835, the Second Seminole War erupted in two simultaneous events. Osceola and a handful of warriors killed Wiley Thompson and a companion outside the gates of Fort King near present-day Ocala. The same day, farther south, Major Francis Dade and his force of more than a hundred soldiers were ambushed by a larger group of Seminole and black warriors. Only three wounded soldiers survived, and just one for more than a few days. These events set in motion the most expensive Indian war ever waged by the US government.

For several months the Seminoles held onto their stronghold at the cove of the Withlacoochee River, repelling army after army. The difficulty of fighting the Seminoles on their turf prompted General Thomas Jesup to conclude, "In regard to the Seminoles, we have committed the error of attempting to remove them when their lands were not required for agricultural purposes; when they were not in the way of white inhabitants; and when the greater

Drawing of Seminole leader Osceola by George Catlin in 1838, Library of Congress.

Seminole Indian reenactor at the Dade Battlefield Historic State Park. The reenactment of the first large battle of the Second Seminole War, when Major Frances Dade and his regiment were wiped out by Seminoles in 1835, occurs the first weekend in January at the state park.

portion of their country was an unexplored wilderness, of the interior of which we were as ignorant as the interior of China."

President Jackson quickly became impatient with the lack of military success achieved by his generals, as expressed in a letter to Florida governor and army general Richard Keith Call in 1836: "For the Lord's sake take some energetic stand, raise your people to action and energy, pursue and destroy every party of Indians that dare approach you. . . . You must act promptly and regain the military fame lost by the wretched conduct of Generals Gaines and Scott. . . . I expect you to act with energy, or you will lose your military fame."

Eventually, the Seminoles were driven from the Cove of the Withlacoochee when large armies approached from three sides. Never again were the Seminoles amassed in such a large concentration. Instead, they dispersed into smaller groups, and most fled to large swamps in the Everglades region. The US Army, in turn, began hunting them down with smaller, more easily deployed forces, often using hounds. Villages and crops were frequently burned, keeping the Seminoles on the run with very little food and few chances to obtain outside supplies and ammunition.

When Osceola was captured under a flag of truce in 1837, Seminole resistance gradually dwindled and band after band of Seminoles began to surrender. Even though a few hundred elusive Seminoles remained in Florida when the United States declared an end to the war in 1842, no treaty was ever signed. The war simply dragged on until hostilities ebbed and most Seminoles, almost four thousand, were shipped west. In all, more than 1,500 US soldiers perished, mostly from disease. Costs were estimated at $30 to $40 million, a huge sum at the time. A third Seminole war occurred in the 1850s after a surveying party raided Chief Billy Bowlegs's garden. As a result, more Seminoles were shipped west. Afterward, about two to three hundred Seminoles held out in the great swamp.

## STORYTELLING TIPS

When you reach the point when the mysterious underwater creatures grab Amanda's ankle and pull her under, inch close enough to an audience member to grab their ankle. Their surprised reaction could add a moment of levity to the story.

**Estimated Telling Time:** 11–12 minutes

# • *15* •

# Lost Village

*W*hile backpacking in the Big Cypress National Preserve in South Florida for a few days, it quickly became apparent that the trails I followed hadn't been cleared in a long time. Brush was thick. Trees had fallen and covered the trail in several places and a recent rainstorm had created several muddy spots. It wasn't easy pushing through, but I was enjoying occasional scenic views of the vast wet prairies and tree islands.

At one point I lost the trail completely and wandered in a large semi-circle, soon stumbling upon a narrow trail that I thought to be the one I needed to follow. It was overgrown just like the others, but in places where I could see the actual ground, I made out small footprints like those made by children. I hadn't seen people all day, so this surprised me. What was even more surprising was that the footprints were smooth. They had no tread marks like you would find from boots or tennis shoes. And a couple of the prints were from bare feet.

Soon, it began to rain, erasing any footprints. I figured there would be some dry ground ahead where I could set up my tent and get out of the weather, so I pressed on. Near dark, the rain stopped, and I was desperate to find a dry clearing. That's when I saw the distant glow of a campfire through the trees with the glimmer of water beyond. Finally! I quickly pressed forward.

What I stumbled upon next was as surprising as anything I had ever seen. It was a small village or camp, a Seminole or Miccosukee Indian village, beside a large pond surrounded by swampland. Several children were running about in colorful traditional patchwork clothing and moccasins, and some were barefoot. Fish were laid on a wood rack over a fire and several open-sided structures with roofs made of palm thatch were situated around it. I knew these to be chickees. When they saw me, everyone froze and stared. A girl

**Traditional Seminole palm-thatched "chickees" at the Ah-Tah-Thi-Ki Museum on the Big Cypress Seminole Reservation in South Florida.**

giggled. A woman's voice barked loudly from the lakeside as she walked up. She spoke to the children in their native tongue and then looked at me hard. With a frown, she said something I didn't understand, sighed, and pointed to a nearby clearing. She pointed her fingers together in a teepee or tent symbol to indicate I could camp there. I nodded and walked to the clearing as several more children giggled.

After I set up my tent, a young boy approached and motioned for me to come to the main camp. There, they gave me smoked fish—a real treat—corn soup and roasted pumpkin. For dessert we had freshly picked berries and sweetened Indian fry bread. "Thank you!" I said warmly, nodding. Some of the children spoke a word or two to me in their native language and giggled. They sure did like to giggle! The woman even smiled too. I looked around, still amazed. I couldn't believe what I was seeing. It was as if nothing had changed for several generations. Was this some sort of time warp?

After supper we sat around the fire and the women told stories in their native language. Some were obviously funny because the children laughed, while others must have had some suspense because a look of concern spread across their bronze-colored faces. At that point I realized that most of the children appeared to be the same age, maybe nine or ten. How odd.

Several of the children began to yawn, and so when they began walking to their huts, I retired to my tent. The next morning at dawn I walked to the pond to brush my teeth. There, I spotted a young girl in braids. Most of the other children were still asleep, I assumed. She had something in her ear—an iPod!

"What have you there?" I asked.

She looked shocked and embarrassed that I had seen her. She quickly glanced toward the huts. "Shhh, I'm not supposed to have this," she said in perfect English. "Tell no one."

"I promise. But what's going on here?"

She bit her lower lip and whispered, "This is a class intensive. We're learning the old ways. We do this every year for a week at this pond. We're not supposed to speak any English, only our native tongue. It's not easy. Many of us know English better than our Indian language."

I nodded, finally understanding. "Your secret is safe with me," I said.

Since it was a sunny morning, I packed my gear and approached the teacher when she emerged from her hut. "Thank you," I said, nodding. "I'll be on my way." I made a walking motion with my fingers. She smiled sweetly, picked up a small stick, and kneeled in front of a cleared area. In the dirt, she drew the pond and village and the trail the led to it. Then she drew a connecting trail that went in another direction—my way out. "Ah," I said. "I see where I took a wrong turn."

Appreciation showed in my eyes for this woman's dedication to her traditions and to her students. With the modern world closing in from every direction, this type of camp could make a lasting impression on these students. Not all of them may want to live in a chickee for the rest of their lives, but maybe they would come to know how to survive in the wilds and have a better appreciation for their heritage. I waved goodbye and left the "lost" village by the pond.

## AUTHOR'S NOTES

While a few Seminole and Miccosukee Indians in South Florida still live in chickees and follow time-honored traditions, most now live in houses and drive vehicles and airboats and speak the English language. Concerned with losing their language and traditional culture, there is a movement among the Seminole Tribe of Florida to teach more of their culture to young people. A charter school that teaches both the English and Seminole language has begun. This story takes traditional education a step further by bringing students to a re-created village for several days to learn the old ways. This is what inspired "Lost Village."

## STORYTELLING TIPS

"Lost Village" is best told with a tone of wonder and amazement, as if a real Seminole village like this really exists.

**Estimated Telling Time:** 7–8 minutes

# · *16* ·

# The Storm

*N*orma cracked open her front door and peered into the storm. Water snakes covered her dirt walkway. All morning, they had been slithering onto her pine island that lay in the middle of a coastal swamp near Cedar Key. She had to shoo the snakes away from her doorway with a stick, but they wouldn't move far. They knew what she now knew. This hurricane was stronger than expected. Rain had begun slanting sideways from the howling wind. Branches, limbs, and pine cones blew past or struck the tin roof in loud thumps. Some trees, bent over by the storm's unrelenting fury, snapped in two or were ripped up from the wet earth. Everywhere, Norma heard the cracking and crashing of limbs and trees.

Norma's husband, Frank, had built the swamp cabin in the 1950s. With the swamp's cabbage palms, lush ferns, and wildflowers, it was the closest they could come to their dream of living in a tropical paradise, like the Caribbean or South Seas. They bought the land for almost nothing and improved an old logging road leading to it. They built most of the cabin from old-growth cypress and pine hauled from the bottom of the Suwannee River, the trees having broken away from log rafts being floated to sawmills at Cedar Key many years before.

At first, the cabin was a weekend spot for them, a welcome retreat from Tampa's hustle and bustle, but when they retired, they moved in full time. When Frank died ten years before, Norma stubbornly remained, ignoring the urgings of friends to move back to the city. She loved the solitude and peaceful feeling of swamp living. She came to regard trees, plants, and animals as friends—to be respected, not feared. In turn, raccoons, possums, deer, alligators, and snakes showed little fear of her. She was not the type to tolerate harm to any creature. That's why she felt the swamp's pain as it was being lashed by the hurricane, but she could do little about it.

The waterway wilderness of Tide Swamp along Florida's Big Bend Coast.

A wild scene in Tide Swamp.

The storm intensified and water began seeping in from under the front door. Norma had raised her furniture on blocks for just such a possibility, and now she was glad she did. The water rose incredibly fast, however. The blocks didn't help; water rose past them and soaked her couch and cabinets and continued rising. Walking in waist-deep water, Norma felt a sense of panic. "Go higher," a voice whispered to her. "Go higher."

Norma had no time to ponder the source of the voice. She realized she had better climb to the crow's nest, the lookout Frank had built atop the roof.

She put on a rain poncho, though she knew it wouldn't do much good in such driving rain and climbed through a window to the outside stairs of the crow's nest. "Hang on tight," the voice whispered again. "Don't worry. You will be safe."

Hugging the railing to keep from being blown off by the wind, she made her way to the deck atop the roof. Though it was daytime, skies were black and ominous looking. Rain pelted her, limiting visibility. She could see enough, however, to know that water was rising around her house and climbing up along the walls. The house shook under the pressure, but thankfully, it did not come apart. Frank had been a good builder.

The crow's nest was atop the center of the roof, the cabin's highest point, and Norma watched with horror as water rose to the tin roofing. Entire trees and logs swirled past. She spotted a deer, trying to swim to her in panic, but it was unable to reach her before being swept along. The water rose to where she felt it cover her feet. The entire roof disappeared under the dark frothing swell. She gripped the rail tighter. "Frank!" she cried. "I'll be coming soon."

A voice answered, whispering to her from the howling wind: "Don't worry, I'm coming for you."

Water rose to her waist. She tried to stay grounded to the crow's nest but she felt herself being lifted by the force of the tidal surge. That's when she saw it through the trees—a small sailboat coming toward her, its mast broken by the storm. It bobbed and careened about, banging into limbs and tree trunks, but its hull seemed sound. The coast was only a short distance away. It must have broken loose from its moorings, she guessed. Norma thought she spotted a man in a dark rain parka guiding the boat, but every time lightning flashed, she saw no one at the helm.

When the boat neared the cabin, she dove for it and climbed aboard with all the strength she had left. She opened the small cabin door and crawled inside, shutting it tightly behind her. Unbelievably, the cabin was dry. She could see the raging storm outside through portholes as the boat rocked up and down, but she dared to feel safe for the first time. She was suddenly very tired. Her breathing became raspy. Her chest felt heavy and her left arm tingled. "Sleep," the voice whispered. "All will be well."

Norma closed her eyes while the boat carried her. She dreamed of sailing down one of the swamp's many wild streams to the Gulf of Mexico. Skies were clear and sunny—blue sky to match blue water—and Norma zoomed across open water at incredible speeds. She eventually landed on a palm-covered island and sandy shores, one with tree-covered hills. Frank was there to meet her. He looked young and vigorous, and miraculously, so did she. "Told you not to worry," he said. "I have everything ready for you."

Frank showed her a beautiful cabin, a tree house of sorts, like in the *Swiss Family Robinson.* A waterfall flowed nearby through a garden of ferns and flowers. Paradise.

"Oh, I wish this were all real!" Norma exclaimed.

Frank smiled. "We can have this place for as long as you want," he said. And from the starlight twinkle in his eyes, she knew it was true.

## AUTHOR'S NOTES

In September 2004, Hurricane Ivan began roaring across the Gulf of Mexico's warm waters, like a gargantuan prairie fire fueled by wind and parched grass. Initially, it was aimed dead center at my home area south of Tallahassee, projected to blast right into Apalachee Bay or slightly west, near Apalachicola. The Gulf of Mexico is like a giant trap once storms enter from the Caribbean. The only escape is to slam into land and wreak havoc.

One forecaster spoke ominously in military terms: "the upcoming assault on the mainland." Another pointed out that the hurricane was ninety miles wide, so devastation could be spread over a huge swath.

Worried friends and relatives called. Some said to leave. Neighbors asked whose house was strongest. We could all hole up in the sturdiest fortress and weather the storm together. My neighbors, Paul and Kristy, have a twenty-eight-sided yurt—designed to steer winds around it. Our friend Kent has outer walls made of a type of cement, perhaps strong enough to withstand heavy winds and falling trees. My parents insisted we stay with them farther inland. "You're closer to the coast," my mother said, worry straining her voice. "You'll get hit harder. Do what is safest."

As the crow flies, the house I share with my wife and daughter is less than twenty miles from the Gulf. We live in low-lying pine flatwoods known as the Woodville coastal plain. Flooding could be a problem, but devastation caused by high winds and falling trees were our main worries.

Everyone we talked with, even friends and family who didn't live in the area, were spooked by the storm. We frequently asked each other: What was there to do besides fill water bottles, buy batteries, and wait?

As we thought about leaving, I worried about the fate of our house, belongings, trees, and pets. It almost seemed traitorous to abandon the place, but was it worth more than my life, or the lives of my wife and daughter?

Even though Hurricane Ivan largely missed us and hit farther west, near Pensacola, the questions that ran through my mind are what millions along the Gulf and Atlantic coasts have asked in recent years as hurricanes bore down on them. This experience helped to spawn "The Storm."

## MORE ABOUT HURRICANES

The first recorded hurricane in the Pensacola area was in 1559 when a killer storm struck only days after two thousand Spanish soldiers and settlers sailed into Pensacola Bay to establish a permanent colony. All but two of the colonists' eleven ships were spared, crippling hopes for further exploration and resupply. The town was soon abandoned and St. Augustine, settled six years later, became the oldest European city on American soil. On November 3, 1752, a hurricane and tidal wave hit Santa Rosa Island and destroyed all buildings of a Spanish settlement there except for a storehouse and hospital.

In September 2005, Hurricane Katrina smashed into Mississippi, Alabama, and Louisiana. Experts began to affirm what many suspected: global warming was helping to intensify hurricanes, worsening the cyclical rise in their frequency.

In Florida, almost every part of the state was affected by deadly hurricanes in 2004 and 2005, but perhaps the Pensacola area was hit the worst. Five named storms struck during that period, Hurricane Ivan being the worst. On the barrier islands of Perdido Key and Santa Rosa Island, roaring winds and high storm surges ripped away nearly all traces of vegetation, and severely damaged or destroyed homes, motels, condominiums, and businesses. The Gulf Islands National Seashore, once an expanse of rolling dunes, shrubs, and coastal forest, resembled a flat barren pancake of white sand. Fort Pickens Campground was closed indefinitely, along with most access roads.

The storm surge swept directly over the islands—a swiftly moving wave of destruction. The aftermath resembled a bombed city and countryside. A year later, cleanup and rebuilding was still in its early stages. Some had completely abandoned hope, their structures eventually demolished or left to the Gulf's lapping waves. Even the National Park Service was questioning the wisdom of pouring more money into a diminishing spit of sand during a period of high hurricane activity and intensity.

Prior to the new millennium, Florida enjoyed a decades-long period of low hurricane frequency, the low ebb of the storm cycle. A building boom resulted. Coastal land prices skyrocketed, and entrepreneurs reaped profits. It goes to show that people, especially planners and decision-makers, often have short memories when it comes to natural disasters, allowing the lessons of history to go unheeded.

From 1877–2005, more than forty-five hurricanes struck within sixty miles of the Pensacola area. That figure alone would seemingly prompt a pause in building or rebuilding along coastal fringes, especially barrier islands, but humans can be stubborn when it comes to living on the beach. Even after the record-setting hurricane season of 2005, coastal counties from Texas to New England continued to grow by more than 1,300 permanent residents a day. "Societal madness," summed up Orrin Pilkey, coastal geologist at Duke University, in *USA Today*. "You have to basically be from Kazakhstan to not understand about shoreline erosion."

In 2016, another cycle of hurricanes began to hit Florida. Hurricane Hermine slammed Florida's upper Gulf Coast. A year later, Hurricane Irma swept through the entire Florida peninsula and in 2018, Hurricane Michael was the largest known storm ever to hit the Florida Panhandle, causing widespread destruction.

According to the United States Environmental Protection Agency, sea level could rise one foot by the year 2050 and from two to four feet by 2100. A chunk of land larger than Massachusetts would be flooded by a two-foot rise. Rising sea levels, coupled with unprecedented hurricane activity, will continue to spell trouble for Florida's coastal areas.

## STORYTELLING TIPS

As the storm surge rises, speed up your storytelling and raise your voice to convey a sense of urgency and panic, but speak with confidence and authority each time the mysterious voice whispers to Norma. Ideal follow-up discussion subjects would be hurricanes, global warming, and sea level rise.

**Estimated Telling Time:** 7–8 minutes

# The Haunted Treasure

$\mathcal{J}$t was dumb luck—finding the treasure of a lifetime by sheer chance.

Bo Crummer was netting mullet in one of many winding tidal creeks along Florida's Big Bend Coast when he noticed something shiny along the shore. The bank of a small island in a marshy expanse had been steadily eroding over time as sea level gradually rose, and when Bo took a closer look, he saw Spanish gold doubloons spilling out from a sandy bank.

Bo knew immediately it was pirate gold, stolen long ago and hidden, eventually lost and forgotten. Stories of buried pirate treasure were common along the Big Bend Coast, but few tales were told of people who found hidden riches.

Immediately after landing his skiff to get a closer look, Bo scanned the horizon. Did anyone else see? He spotted no one. No boats, planes, or people. Only a wild coastline of marsh, cabbage palm, cedar, and live oak.

Bo pulled out a handful of garbage bags, doubled them up, and began filling them with the gold. Only a few doubloons lay in the mud. Most were concentrated in one part of the embankment as if they had once been encased in a wooden chest that had since rotted away. He filled three doubled-up bags and knotted them tight. They were heavy, very heavy. And priceless. Once on board, Bo did a little jig. "Har!" he cried out in his best pirate voice. An osprey whistled as if to join the celebration.

Generations of Bo's family had fished this remote segment of the Gulf Coast since the Civil War. They had always been poor, living in tin-roofed shacks that were sometimes blown apart by hurricanes, but they had never gone hungry. The sea always provided, but with new fishing regulations, Bo had found it increasingly difficult to make a living. Not anymore. He might never have to fish again!

**Marsh and water scene along Florida's Big Bend Coast.**

A thousand thoughts raced through his head on the way back to the docks. He would keep the treasure secret—too many government regulations otherwise, and people who would want to get their hands on it. He wouldn't know whom to trust. He'd find a way to cash in the doubloons little by little over time at different places. He'd say he found them on the beach or that a relative discovered them years before.

Bo figured he would have to hold back from buying too many things, like a new truck or house. Otherwise, he would arouse suspicion. People would think he was smuggling drugs. Then the law would be after him, and the Internal Revenue Service. Yes, he'd have to be careful, very careful, and still do some fishing, or pretend to have an inland job part of the year when he and his family would be on some exotic vacation, like in Hawaii. He always wanted to go to Hawaii.

Suddenly, the boat lurched sideways, hit by an unexpected gust of wind. Where did that come from? Bo wondered. The sea was calm as glass.

At the dock no one seemed to notice that Bo's face was flushed, or that his heart beat faster than normal. He was sure everyone would know about his find by just looking at him, but there were only occasional nods and the usual comments about weather, fish prices, and upcoming high school football games. Nothing was mentioned of pirate treasure.

Bo unloaded his mullet in plastic buckets, weighed them at the fish house, and collected his money. "Small catch for you this time of year," was the only comment Mr. Barfield made. Bo tried to look sad as he nodded in agreement. Inside, however, he was about to burst. This was his lucky day. He had found the treasure of a lifetime, his biggest catch of all, and he couldn't tell anyone.

Trying to look casual, Bo hoisted one gold-filled bag at a time from his boat to his faded pickup truck. He sweated profusely, more out of nervousness than from heat or exertion. He drove quickly and pulled up closer to his house than usual, under the shade of a live oak. For seemingly the first time, he noticed how paint on the old cypress siding was faded and chipped, having been battered by storms and salt spray. He would get a new paint job, he vowed, and a new roof, and build an addition, and install a swimming pool in the backyard, and—. He cut off his thoughts. *Don't be greedy*, he told himself. Patience. He would do things gradually, in small steps.

He hauled the bags inside the house and to the bedroom. No one was home. His wife Melinda worked in an oyster house, prying open the hard shells and scooping meat into containers. It was brutal on the hands. She could quit soon, work part-time somewhere else—an easy job, like at the new library. She'd never have to get her hands dirty or nicked again.

Bo's two children, Bonnie and Tad, were nine and ten years old and still at school. They could get new clothes, and shiny bikes, and—he checked his thoughts again. Patience. Patience.

Dropping to his knees before the main closet, Bo shoved boots and shoes aside and slid the black bags along the floor to the back wall. Once in place, curiosity got the best of him. He had to touch the gold again. He had not eaten lunch, never even gave it a thought, and his hands quivered from hunger and adrenaline. When he untied the double knot, he reached in and pulled out a handful of doubloons. Even in the shadows, they seemed to sparkle. Gold! Through the ages, people went crazy over the precious yellow metal, even killed for it. *This is unbelievable*, he thought to himself. Unbelievable! And he had just stumbled upon it. He must surely be the luckiest man alive.

Bo put the doubloons into his pocket. Even this little bit was worth a small fortune, he guessed. He would show it to Melinda when she got home. He'd have to stop her from screaming with excitement and make her vow to keep it secret. It wouldn't be easy in a small town, but he trusted she would. The alternative was several more years shucking oysters.

Feeling the jingle of coins in his pocket, Bo strode to the kitchen. He felt very hungry. He placed a frozen hamburger in a frying pan and turned on the gas burner. He munched on potato chips and gulped a soda, unable to sit still. He walked around the house in small circles. He couldn't stop thinking of things he could buy with the gold.

When Bo flipped the sizzling hamburger, he heard a knock at the door. *Not now*, he thought. He didn't want visitors, or salespeople. The knock was persistent. Reluctantly, Bo answered it. Standing in the doorway was a stranger, a red-bearded man in rumpled clothes and bare feet. A bum, Bo determined, and a smelly bum, but Bo also noticed the leathery skin of someone who had spent countless days on the water. He was likely a fisherman or sailor down on his luck.

"Yeah, can I help you?" Bo said, trying to be polite. He'd give the man some money and food, he determined, just to get him to leave. After all, he now had a bit extra to share. He managed a smile.

"Hey mister, I need to tell you something," the stranger announced. He sounded hoarse, as though something was stuck in his throat.

The bum smelled so bad Bo didn't want to invite him into the house, so he stepped out. "Yeah, I got a little time, but my lunch is cooking," he said. His eyes studied the long scar on the man's cheek, likely made by a knife blade, he thought.

"This won't take long," the man said.

Bo cleared his throat. "You want something to eat?"

The man shook his head and began, "There was this pirate, see, a long time ago, and he had to find a place to bury his treasure."

Bo shook from a sudden chill. He felt frozen to the porch.

The man continued, "This pirate, he went up one of them creeks and followed the smoke plume straight north, the one that came from the swamps, the one that never stopped. Some called it the devil's tar-kiln."

"The Wakulla Volcano?" Bo interjected. He had heard stories all his life about the unending column of smoke that once rose from the swamps around the Wacissa, Aucilla, and Wakulla Rivers, one where a tall arch of flame could occasionally be spotted over the treetops. It was seen for centuries, written about by Spanish sailors and early settlers of the Tallahassee area. People called it the Wakulla Volcano. Many adventurers attempted to find it, but no one did. The swamps were too impenetrable. Some said the smoke was from an Indian campfire. Others said it was a smoldering peat fire or a natural gas vent that had caught fire.

Bo smelled his hamburger burning on the stove. "Uhh, I need to go in and—."

"The pirate," continued the stranger more strongly, "would sail back to his treasure when he saw fit—add to it or take from it. He'd find it by following the smoke plume. Then one year, right after the earth shook and rang church bells from here to St. Augustine, the smoke disappeared and never came back, and the pirate couldn't find his treasure anymore. He searched, and searched, and searched." The man's voice revealed a hint of exasperation.

Bo tried to keep from shaking. He had heard that the Wakulla Volcano vanished after the 1886 Charleston earthquake rocked the southeastern United States. "So, what does all this have to do with—?"

As quickly as a shark strikes at its prey, the stranger lunged toward Bo. He grabbed his hair and tilted his head back. Bo glimpsed a cold knife being held to his throat. The long blade was silver and curved, inlaid with jewels. "Now matey," the man rasped, "don't play coy with me. You can keep what's in your pocket. After all, this is your lucky day. But the rest is mine! Give back me treasure!"

Bo couldn't speak. He felt depleted of all air. "Cat got your tongue?" the man asked, smiling.

Bo managed to nod. The stranger took a step back. Bo took a breath. "I'll get it for you," he managed to say.

"That'd be smart."

Bo shuffled into the living room and made his way to the bedroom closet. As he pulled out the bags, he opened one of them and dipped a hand into it, pulling out several doubloons. A few more in the pocket wouldn't hurt, he thought. He also glanced at the .22 rifle in the corner and began to reach for it. Suddenly, he felt the knife at his throat again. "That wouldn't be too smart, would it?" Bo nodded in agreement, putting the coins back. He was surprised at how quietly the man had snuck up on him. "Help me carry it outside," the man ordered.

Bo dragged two bags while the man hoisted the other over a shoulder with surprising strength. Bo followed the man to a narrow tidal creek at the end of the road. A small, decrepit dinghy had been hoisted onto the marshy shore. "Put it in there," the man ordered. Bo did as he was told, feeling the pricks of needlerush on his arms. With the treasure in the boat, the man stepped in and pushed off. He said, "Here's something for your troubles, matey." He flipped Bo a gold doubloon. It spun in the air, glinting from sunlight. Bo caught it. It felt cold in his hands. The man laughed then, a long hearty laugh. "I got me treasure back," he cried. "I got me treasure!"

As Bo watched him paddle down the creek toward the Gulf, he could swear he saw a narrow plume of smoke over the horizon, as if it had always been there.

## AUTHOR'S NOTES

Having moved to Florida's Big Bend region when I was eleven, it wasn't long before I heard tales about the mysterious Wakulla Volcano once visible from Tallahassee's hills. What was it? I always wondered. An Indian or runaway slave camp? A smoldering peat bog? Moonshiners? A real spouting volcano?

The "volcano," combined with a boyhood fascination with pirates—many of whom utilized the Big Bend's remote rivers and islands to bury their treasures—helped to make "The Haunted Treasure" come alive.

## MORE ABOUT THE WAKULLA VOLCANO

Building upon stories handed down by Spaniards and American Indians, the Wakulla Volcano was the rave of Tallahassee soon after the city was founded in 1824. People talked about it as much as the weather. On a clear day, the tall column of smoke could be spotted from rooftops and from the capitol rotunda. The smoke plume was even more visible from Apalachee Bay, along the Gulf of Mexico.

In 1997, Pete Gerrell of the Woodville area wrote about the Wakulla Volcano in the *Tallahassee Democrat* in 1997: "My great-great-grandfather John Costello, and his brother, Antonio, piloted sailing ships between New Orleans and Tampa, carrying supplies in and out of the St. Marks River. . . . Word of mouth passed down through the generations is that they used the smoke column from the volcano as the signal that they were almost home."

Interestingly, the smoke was said to change color, from white to black and various shades in between. At night, some said they could see a fiery glow coming from the "volcano."

Numerous people tried to find the source of the smoke—both before and after it disappeared—to no avail. One newspaper reporter in the 1870s allegedly perished during a strenuous volcano searching expedition through a watery tangle of swamplands.

A *New York Times* reporter wrote this account of the Wakulla Volcano in 1880:

> It is much brighter some nights than others—sometimes having the appearance of the moon rising, but generally much brighter, and looking more like a large fire shooting its flaming tongue high up into the upper realms, frequently reflected back by passing clouds. During the past week we have conversed with several parties living in that direction, all of whom had noticed the light, and located it in the great swamp southeast of here, on

the Gulf coast, and about the same spot from whence the much-talked-of column of black smoke has been seen to issue for years, supposed to be a volcano, which no living man has ever been able to reach, from the fact of its being surrounded by an impenetrable swamp.

An article written in 1883 in *The Florida Dispatch* adds to the mystery: "This column of smoke has existed and been seen by the oldest inhabitants of the county for the past fifty years. Indeed, it was so constantly visible, that during the war the blockading vessels became suspicious of its being a Rebel camp for the manufacture of arms and ammunition, and on several occasions threw shells at it."

Following the 1886 Charleston earthquake, when the smoke plume disappeared, explorers near the Pinhook River reportedly found a small black crater with a bottom too deep to fathom.

Two businessmen in the early 1930s searched in earnest for the volcano, following directions left by a nineteenth-century Chicago newsman who had perhaps gotten closer to the smoke column than anyone. "We were crazy!" recalls William Wyatt, one of the two explorers, in a 1964 *Tallahassee Democrat* article. "We started out in a Model T Ford with a machete, a hand-ax, a flashlight, and a small bag of sandwiches."

After hacking their way through a swamp, the men found piles of rocks that appeared to have been "blown out of the ground." Wyatt concludes, "There was something eerie about the place because there were no trees as in the surrounding land, yet it had never been logged because there were no stumps."

In 1997, Tallahassee radio personality Sonny Branch claimed to have found the original source of the "volcano." He led a group down a rut-filled road just inside Jefferson County through a swamp known as Hell's Half Acre. *Tallahassee Democrat* reporter Kathleen Laufenberg describes the scene when the entourage finally stopped, "The swamp's green arms entwine everywhere around the land, making it nearly impenetrable. . . . But at least from the road, there is no crater to be seen. No giant boulders. Nothing that dramatically sets this piece of swamp apart from any other within a ten-mile radius."

Branch concluded that the "volcano" was a peat-bog fire that started in one place and spread through different types of vegetation, thus the reason the smoke changed color. Geologists in the group remained skeptical. Today, tales of the Wakulla Volcano continue to instill a sense of awe and mystery in listeners, just as the real column of smoke did with American Indians, Spanish explorers, pirates, mariners, and early Tallahassee residents.

## STORYTELLING TIPS

A pivotal moment in the story is when the pirate holds a curved and jeweled knife to Bo's throat, demanding the treasure. You should be able to obtain a plastic pirate-style knife at a toy store, glue on fake jewels, and use it as a prop to reenact this scene. Dressing up like a pirate and invoking phrases such as "Harrrrr!" also helps to bring this story to life. Optional props include chocolate coins wrapped in gold foil that can be distributed to your audience afterward, a warm gesture of treasure sharing.

**Estimated Telling Time:** 13–14 minutes

# Ghost Bird

*I*'m not sure what lured me to the Aucilla bottomlands, a wide swampy area just below where the Aucilla River reemerges from underground after disappearing into a huge sinkhole. To get there by land, and I use the word "land" loosely, I began walking down the Florida Trail just south of Highway 98.

I soon began questioning the wisdom of going hiking only five days after a heavy Christmas rain. I waded in knee-deep icy water in places more than I hiked. The water flowed down the trail in one spot as it sought lower ground. Its dark tint often hid limestone boulders lurking just under the surface. There were also biting mosquitoes—in December!

When I reached the long-abandoned railroad tram in the St. Marks National Wildlife Refuge, I headed east toward the Aucilla River while the Florida Trail veered west. There was no trail where I went. The old rail bed was overgrown with sable palms and river cane. The first bridge was long gone, and so I waded across the watery expanse, past cypress and gum trees with their swollen bases, frequently pausing. An eagle cried—I saw its silhouette against the blue sky.

Then my attention was riveted to sounds of a creature splashing through the swamp. I half expected to see a lumbering bear since this was one of their domains, but I soon spied a solid brown and very wet wild boar about knee high. He passed me, forty yards away, never once looking my way. I felt relieved.

This was no longer a place for man, I realized. Loggers had cut the big swamp trees about eighty years ago and hauled them out with steam locomotives, but young trees gradually filled in the gaps, and the Aucilla bottomlands had become wild again. I only wished the loggers could have left just a few of the original cypress, many of which were hundreds and thousands of years old.

These old trees had been Florida's version of the California redwoods—some grew as wide as dump trucks and as tall as cell phone towers.

The second bridge span along the tram was also missing. Navigating around the watery expanse was trickier, with more sucking mud. By the time I reached the third bridgeless expanse, with no clear way around—only deep, dark water—I checked my watch. Three o'clock. Sunset was around five-thirty, and it took me two hours to get to this point. I had no flashlight, and I was alone. A half hour is a small margin of error when alone in the wilds. What if I was attacked by a wild boar, or sprained an ankle?

Just when I was about to turn around, that's when I saw it—a large woodpecker about twenty inches long with white wing patches and a light-colored bill. An ivory-billed! This was North America's largest and rarest woodpecker species, long considered extinct until some claimed to have spotted one in an Arkansas swamp in 2004. Historically, some have called it "the Lord God Bird" because eyewitness observers have exclaimed, "Lord God, what a bird!"

Millions of birdwatchers have longed to see an ivory-billed woodpecker. To spot an ivory-bill is like finding Elvis and all four Beatles jamming together in your living room. In Florida, the birds were believed to have disappeared with the old swamp trees they depended upon. Nearly all the original forests were logged, but somehow this bird must have hung on in the Aucilla bottomlands of the St. Marks refuge, where few people ever roam.

The woodpecker flew directly from one cypress to the next, occasionally rapping on a trunk with a loud hammer-like sound and peeling away bark in a search for insects. I decided to follow the bird, no matter what. I waded and swam and pushed my way through the swamp and keeping the bird in sight. And then, at a spot where many old cypress trees had formed a type of ring, the bird made a call that sounded like the toot of a tin horn. It rapped twice on a trunk. Then, unbelievably, it swooped to another ivory bill perched on a limb. They briefly clasped bills together. Is this how ivory-bills kissed?

I couldn't believe my luck. The birds zoomed in and out of a nest cavity in a large cypress. This was incredible. No one had witnessed such a scene in seventy or eighty years!

Pulling out my small pocket camera, one that had a built-in zoom lens, I took a few good shots. Then I began to wonder: Whom should I tell? If I shared my discovery with the world, this place would be overrun with birdwatchers. Then, the ivory-bills, who seemed to have gotten along fine without people all these years, wouldn't be able to get away from them. I suddenly felt a strong sense of responsibility.

Before the day grew too late, I waded out of the swamp, walking the last half mile in twilight as temperatures dropped. I whistled happily. Images of the

Ivory-billed woodpeckers as depicted by John James Audubon in the early 1800s, Library of Congress.

two ivory-bills were still strong in my mind. They warmed me and seemed to light my way. I was filled with awe. Where did the birds go when this place was logged back in the 1920s?

I quickly downloaded the photos from my camera and nervously viewed them. Several good shots came out. I double-checked my bird book. The clear images were unmistakably ivory-billed woodpeckers. White patches on their wings immediately told a knowledgeable person that these were not pileated woodpeckers, their close but common relatives. Anyone who knew anything about birding would go crazy if they saw them. Plus, the photos had a date stamped in the corner, proof that these were recent photos.

After careful consideration, I decided to tell my friend Mike, who works as a biologist with the St. Marks National Wildlife Refuge. I insisted on speaking to him alone and made him promise not to tell anyone until we both agreed on a plan. "Why am I making this promise?" he kept asking.

"Because you have to," I said, "or I won't tell you my secret."

He finally nodded. "Oh okay, I promise, but you better not be pulling my leg."

I opened the gallery and showed him the photos; his eyes got as wide as saucers. "Where in the world did you take these?"

"The Aucilla bottomlands. I saw a male and female pair, but there must be more."

"Unbelievable. This is really unbelievable. We thought if there were ivory-bills on the refuge, that's where they'd have to be, but we never really believed it could be possible." He shook his head and his jaw hung open for the third time. "This is really unbelievable," he said again.

"I'll take you there," I offered.

"You'd better. This is a miracle. If we find them, we'd better contact the Cornell Lab of Ornithology. They'll know what to do."

The next morning Mike made some excuse about having to do a bear survey and we set off for the Aucilla bottomlands. The water hadn't subsided much, and we did a lot of wading and pushing through brush. The day was sunny, the landmarks seemed clear, and my compass worked fine, but even though I was sure I knew where I was going, I couldn't find that special grove of old cypress trees, or the ivory-bills. We searched and searched.

"But they were here," I kept saying. "Right in this area. And the trees were old, big, and magnificent."

"Hmmm," said Mike skeptically. "I don't remember ever seeing old-growth cypress in here. I think they were all cut decades ago."

"But you've seen the photos," I replied. "They couldn't have been manipulated on a computer, and I took the shots right around here. I'm sure of it. And the photos are still in my camera and on my computer."

Mike simply shook his head. He knew me well enough to know I wasn't a practical joker, or someone going out of my way to seek attention. So he kept searching with me—for a solid week. We spotted two black bears and a dozen wild pigs, but no ivory-bills. Mike wanted to examine the photos again. They might provide more clues. That's when another strange thing happened. They were blank. Both photos were blank! Only the date remained in the corner. So we checked my camera and computer, and they were blank too. Without them, I would likely be viewed as just another wishful thinker who had mistaken a common pileated woodpecker for an ivory-bill. Understandably, Mike had to move onto other work. "If you find the birds again," he said, sighing, "don't call me."

I was left to ponder the mystery alone. Perhaps swamps do not reveal their secrets easily, I concluded.

Deciding to search one last time, I waded to the spot I thought I had visited the first time, and somehow—like a miracle—I found the special grove of old cypress trees again, and the ivory-billed woodpeckers. Mike and I must have hiked to that spot several times, I was sure, so what was going on?

I watched the ivory-bills fly and call to each other and rap on trees as if they were drums. This was too strange, I thought.

That night I dreamed about the special ring of old cypress trees and the rare birds. A voice spoke to me, seeming to come from the very swamp itself: "This is how it was; this is how it could be again. It is up to us, and it is up to you to make it happen."

## AUTHOR'S NOTES

A momentous year for birdwatchers was 2004. Experts claimed that a bird once thought extinct—the ivory-billed woodpecker—had been seen and photographed in the wild river swamps of eastern Arkansas. The incredible news prompted me to wonder: Where in Florida might ivory-bills be found? A natural conclusion was the remote and wild Aucilla River bottomlands in the St. Marks National Wildlife Refuge, a recovering swamp wilderness area that had once harbored ivory-billed woodpeckers. The rare bird was reportedly spotted here in 1959.

"Ghost Bird" is a "What if" story. What if a verified sighting of the ivory-billed woodpecker was reported in Florida? One can dream that it could happen.

## MORE ABOUT THE IVORY-BILLED
## WOODPECKER AND CYPRESS FORESTS

The ivory-bill was the largest woodpecker north of Mexico and the third largest in the world. Inhabiting mature swamp forests, it roamed large areas in search of standing dead and dying trees infested with beetle larvae, its primary food. They also fed on fruits and nuts. Alexander Wilson, an early naturalist, described the ivory-bill this way: "In these almost inaccessible recesses, amid ruinous piles of impending timber, his trumpet-like note and loud strokes resound through the solitary savage wilds, of which he seems the sole lord and inhabitant."

According to the Cornell Lab of Ornithology, the ivory-bill is,

> 18 to 20 inches tall, it has a wingspan of 30 to 31 inches and weighs 16 to 20 ounces. The bird has a jet black body with large white patches on the wings. A white stripe extends from below each yellow-colored eye, down the sides of the neck and onto the sides of its back. When the wings are folded, it appears that there is a large "shield" of white on the lower back of an ivory-bill. The males have a brilliant red color at the back of their crests, which curves back, whereas the females have a black crest that curves forward.

Unlike the undulating flight characteristic of other woodpeckers, an ivory-bill's was strong and direct and they preferred to fly above trees for long distances travel rather than navigate through branches. Experts such as James Tanner, who researched ivory-bills in the 1930s, believed that a breeding pair of ivory-bills required a suitable territory of about six square miles. They would live twenty to thirty years long. Tanner observed that ivory-bills exhibited a characteristic double-knock when striking a tree, possibly to communicate with other ivory-bills, and their call resembled the tooting of a tin horn. According to the Cornell Lab, ivory-bills "begin breeding in January, laying an average of three eggs per clutch. Both parents care for the young. Ivory-billed Woodpeckers fledge at about five weeks of age and may remain dependent on their parents for a year or more."

The ivory-billed woodpecker began to hover on the brink of extinction with the disappearance of the old-growth hardwood trees they depended upon. One of the last documented sightings in Florida was in 1949 when birdwatcher Whitney Eastman and his search team claimed to have spotted a pair of ivory-bills in a remote floodplain swamp along the Chipola River. "It was the greatest thrill of my bird-watching life," Eastman was quoted in a 1950 issue of *Florida Wildlife*. Soon afterward, two more birds were spotted. With cooperation from lumber companies who owned the land, the Florida

Fish and Wildlife Conservation Commission set aside the area as a 1,300-acre bird sanctuary. Unfortunately, when no additional sightings were reported, the sanctuary status was discontinued in 1952.

In the 1950s and 1960s, other sightings in Florida by credible ornithologists and birdwatchers occurred in Collier County near Big Cypress Swamp, south of Tallahassee in Wakulla County, Homosassa Springs, the western side of the Aucilla River, near Eglin Air Force Base in the Panhandle, the Green Swamp, and northwest of Lake Okeechobee. After 1970, ivory-bills were reportedly spotted in Cuba, Texas, Louisiana, Mississippi, Alabama, and Georgia, but it wasn't until 2004 that events unfolded to shake the birdwatching world. Reported sightings of ivory-bills occurred in The Big Woods of eastern Arkansas, the first sighting in that area since 1910. A short video was released. "The bird captured on video is clearly an Ivory-billed Woodpecker," concluded John Fitzpatrick, director of the Cornell Lab of Ornithology. "Amazingly, America may have another chance to protect the future of this spectacular bird and the awesome forests in which it lives."

The birdwatching furor began when kayaker Gene Sparling claimed he spotted what he believed to be an ivory-billed woodpecker during a float trip through the Big Woods in late February 2004. A week later, Sparling guided two expert birders into the area, Tim Gallagher and Bobby Harrison. While Sparling paddled ahead, a large black and white woodpecker flew across the bayou in front of Gallagher and Harrison. Both simultaneously cried out: "Ivory-bill!" They immediately sketched what they had seen, and afterward, Harrison was overcome with emotion and began sobbing, saying, "I saw an ivory-bill. I saw an ivory-bill."

"Just to think this bird made it into the twenty-first century gives me chills," said Gallagher. "It's like a funeral shroud has been pulled back, giving us a glimpse of a living bird, rising Lazarus-like from the grave." Subsequent searches that year resulted in fifteen reported sightings of an ivory-bill in the area, but no photographic proof.

The reported rediscovery prompted renewed efforts to protect more of Arkansas' Big Woods, estimated to cover 550,000 acres, and larger teams of researchers were sent out in search of breeding pairs and active nest cavities. Other areas of the South, including Florida's Choctawhatchee and Wacissa and Aucilla river swamps, were identified as potential ivory-bill habitats.

## STORYTELLING TIPS

For a dedicated birder, to spot an ivory-billed woodpecker is equivalent to a treasure-hunter finding a cache of gold. The heart begins to race, and emotion and excitement overcomes the observer. When telling this story, fill your voice with a sense of wonder and awe when the rare ivory-bills are spotted.

**Estimated Telling Time:** 11–12 Minutes

# · *19* ·

# Lost

$\mathcal{I}$ received a writing assignment from a forestry magazine to find world-record-sized trees in Bradwell Bay, a massive swamp in North Florida's Apalachicola National Forest. The bay was named after a hunter who got lost in the area in the 1800s.

Part of Bradwell Bay had never been logged, mainly because early loggers got bogged down in the wet terrain, so some of the remaining trees were huge. Two of those trees were the world's largest Ogeechee tupelo gum trees, a species that grows in southern swamps and along rivers. Many people believed that more world-record sized trees could be found in Bradwell Bay. So I hiked several miles into the heart of the swamp, often wading in waist-deep water. I had a measuring tape and notebook to record my findings.

Everything was going fine until I stepped into a deep underwater hole and fell. Panicked, I swam and thrashed around in the dark water and muck until I regained my footing. Once I caught my breath, I realized I had lost both my compass and my hand-held GPS unit that was helping me find my way. They were somewhere in the black water, lying at the bottom of Bradwell Bay. The sky was overcast, so I couldn't use the sun to navigate. I quickly became lost.

When you're lost in a swamp, the whole environment takes on a spooky air. Tangles of vines weave death-like grips around trees. Moving shadows resemble lurking phantoms. Around any bend you expect to encounter a water moccasin, alligator, or bear. I had seen where bears had clawed trees to mark their territories. Bradwell Bay, being twenty-five thousand acres of wild country, had numerous black bears.

I also worried about stepping into more deep spots in the swamp, places that might suck me under like quicksand.

A hiker wades through the wet wilderness of Bradwell Bay.

As the cloudy sky darkened, I knew the sun was setting. I became more frightened. I had no flashlight. I was cold and wet. The only dry ground was around mossy bases of gum and cypress trees where leaves had built up over time—not enough room to lie down. Mosquitoes whined in my ears. I walked into several spider webs.

Soon, everything around me became dark, very dark—there was no moon. No stars shone through the trees. The night became filled with whirring cicadas, choruses of tree frogs, and a lone hooting owl. Occasionally, I would jump when an animal splashed through the swamp. At one point, I heard a deep grunt from what I assumed to be a bear as it caught my scent. I had nothing to use as a weapon, only a small pocketknife. I relied on the fact that Florida black bears have never been known to attack people, even helpless ones in the dark. But who would ever know? Eventually, the creature left.

As thunder rumbled in the distance and a light rain began to fall, I decided to sit quietly on one of the mossy tree bases. It wasn't very large, so I had to leave my feet sitting in the water. My body shivered from cold and fear. There was no place to make a fire, nor did I have matches or a lighter. I felt like crying, feeling lower than when I had struck out with bases loaded in the bottom of the last inning in a Little League game. I felt lonely then, even among a crowd of people. But I felt lonelier now.

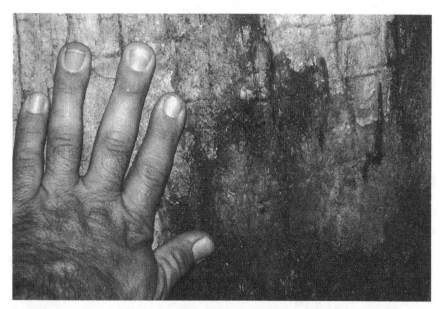

**Bear claw marks on a tree in the Bradwell Bay Wilderness Area in North Florida.**

I gulped down my last granola bar and closed my eyes, hoping I could sleep but knowing it was unlikely. I worried about becoming too chilled and dying from hypothermia. I couldn't stop shaking. I didn't want this to be the last night of my life, but what else could I do?

Somewhere around what I thought was midnight, during my shivering, swatting of mosquitoes, and snatches of sleep, I began to see something odd. In the distance, weaving in and out of the dark shapes of tree trunks, I spotted a small light. It was a yellowish and flickering, not a flashlight-type beam, and it came toward me slowly. The sound of someone or something sloshing through the water grew louder and the light became brighter. It was soon apparent that the light was a small flame from inside an old-fashioned oil lantern, and holding it was a man in rumpled clothes and a floppy wide-brimmed hat. In the man's other hand was a weathered musket, much like the one hanging on my wall at home from my great-great grandfather. "How do?" came a deep voice. I felt a chill.

"Hello," I responded.

"You ready?"

"Ready for what?"

The man waved a hand, turned, and began walking away. "You want me to follow?" I asked. The man said nothing. He just kept walking. I decided to quit asking questions and follow. What did I have to lose?

The man walked incredibly fast. I almost had to run through the water to keep up. Lightning flashed and my rescuer momentarily disappeared before reappearing. Did I only imagine that?

I pushed through vines and tripped over fallen branches, but I was determined not to lose sight of that light. Then I began to wonder: Who was this man? How did he find me? And most disturbing of all: What if he wasn't rescuing me? What if I had died and he was leading me to some other place, a place for lost souls?

I abruptly stopped and yelled, "I'm not going another step until you tell me who you are and where you're taking me!" I tried to keep my teeth from chattering.

The man tensed, glanced back, and shone the lantern on me. "Suit yourself," he said, and continued walking. As darkness closed in around me, I realized I didn't need to know answers to my questions after all. I hurried to catch up. Lightning flashed, and my rescuer momentarily disappeared again before reappearing.

We must have hiked and waded for two hours until we reached a pine forest bordering the great swamp. This was dry ground. I felt relieved, but the man didn't pause. He just kept moving, never growing tired, it seemed. My stomach growled from hunger, my leg muscles were burning, but I raced along behind him. At least the exercise was warming me up, and being out of the water, I no longer feared dying of hypothermia, assuming I was still alive. Even the night sky was clearing. I could make out the Pleiades.

A rustle in the brush prompted the man to stop. "Blue!" he called. "Blue, you out there?" Whatever it was, it stopped moving, and we heard nothing else. The man sighed and continued his fast pace.

We were soon walking on a familiar trail that led to a dirt road. Eventually I could see the silhouette of my car. My mysterious guide stopped then. He turned to me slowly and I got a good look at his face—old and grizzled, with a long beard and sad brown eyes. "Best you be on your way now," he said.

"But what about you?"

He glanced back toward the swamp. "Lost my dog," he said. "Been searching a long time. Can't leave until I find him."

I didn't argue, I was so relieved to get out of that swamp. The man turned halfway and halted, as if remembering something. He fumbled in his pocket. "Here, I believe these are yours." With cold hands, he gave me the compass and GPS unit I had lost. "There's still some big trees in thar," he said. "Used to be a lot more."

"Thank you," I stuttered. "Thank you very much. What's your name, friend?"

"Name is Bradwell," he said. "And I lost my dog."


## AUTHOR'S NOTES


Like many of my stories, I like to merge fact with fiction. Bradwell Bay is a real place with world-record sized tupelo gum trees. I once explored the area for *American Forests* magazine, my assignment being to find the old-growth trees. A forester told me the approximate location: "Follow the Florida Trail until you reach the heart of the swamp, and when the trail veers to the right, keep going straight until you find them." I took my father along, and as we wandered off the marked trail on a cold winter's morning, following a compass and wading up to our thighs, the thought occurred to me that without the compass, we could easily get lost—and then what? Where would we spend the night? How could we build a fire? How would we find our way out? I didn't envy old Bradwell, the poor lost hunter for whom the swamp was named in the 1800s.

I've been lost in the woods before, though never in a swamp, but the feeling of panic that emerges is the same.

World record Ogeechee tupelo tree in the heart of the Bradwell Bay Wilderness.

## MORE ABOUT FINDING YOUR WAY

When you think of all the fun things you can do in Florida's outdoors—hiking, biking, hunting, horseback riding, boating, fishing—becoming lost is probably not one of them. That is, unless you really enjoy the sensation of heart palpitations, sweaty palms, and a rock-hard feeling in your stomach. These simple suggestions can help you find your way in the wilds:

*Maps:* If traveling in unfamiliar territory, up-to-date maps and guidebooks are essential. Government agencies are good sources for maps of areas they manage, and they are often free. Be leery of maps that "friends" scratch out for you on box tops or in the dirt. Staying on a marked trail is also a good precaution.

*Go with a group:* Most local newspapers post listings of outings in your area and you can often find contact information for outdoor groups at your local library. Plus, if you're a single adult, group outings are a great way to meet other single people with similar interests. Just remember, there is no better way to ruin a first date than to get lost.

*Essential supplies:* Even for a day trip, bring a compass, first-aid kit, rain poncho, knife, whistle, small mirror for signaling, water purification tablets, flashlight, lighter, toilet paper, and plenty of water and snacks. An emergency space blanket isn't a bad idea either. GPS is useful if you know how to use one. Make sure you take a reading from your embarking point and mark it "home." Bear in mind, however, that GPS units can be finicky in a thick forest canopy, and batteries can run low. Make sure you have a backup compass.

Cell phones can be useful, but they can also lead to a false sense of security. Reception may be limited in a wilderness area. Rescuers have found that people are calling for help with cell phones when they are simply becoming a little tired or hot. A rescue may cost several hundred dollars or more, and you might be charged for it.

*Leave word:* A simple note on the kitchen table that says "going hiking" doesn't leave many clues for rescuers to follow. A map or detailed description with an estimated time of return would be more useful. Take this precaution even if going with a partner. What if your partner is the one who gets you lost?

*Check the weather forecast:* Check the weather before departing and prepare for foul weather even if the rain chance is low. Don't just glance at the sky and conclude that everything will be fine.

*Call ahead:* Land and water managers can inform you of special conditions in the area you plan on visiting. Perhaps there is a trail closure or storm damage. Be sure to wear hunter orange if traveling through areas open to hunting.

*Observe landmarks:* Try to observe and memorize landmarks, whether they are buoys, docks, fungus, or tree stands. Also, periodically glance back to see how those landmarks might appear on the return trip.

*Don't panic:* If lost, frequently pause to take deep breaths and calm yourself. Realize that it could be worse. You could be trudging across arctic tundra with the ice breaking up and your sled dogs end up on one chunk of ice and you're on the other. Or you might have just realized that the leaves you used for toilet paper were not from a tree but from poison ivy. Or the animal following you for the last two miles that you assumed was your little dog "Spot" has just let out a deep-throated grunt. Things could always be worse, so try to retrace your movements. Avoid taking shortcuts through unfamiliar territory in order to save time.

If you can't retrace your steps, break out your compass (if you brought one), focus on a landmark, and move toward it. Once you've achieved this, focus on the next landmark. This will prevent you from walking in circles. In most Florida wild areas, you'll come across some sign of civilization—such as a road—within a few hours. If you find a road, trail, or river, follow it and stay with it. It is best not to walk at night, however, and stay put if you feel you are wandering aimlessly. Find an open spot and try to make a fire. Three fires spaced thirty or forty feet apart in a triangle is a signal for help to passing aircraft.

## STORYTELLING TIPS

If you've ever been lost, even for a short while, it is difficult to subdue the growing sense of panic and urgency. Try to convey that feeling in this story as you describe getting lost in the swamp and having to spend the night. Then, alternate from relief to doubt to desperation as the ghostly rescuer arrives and begins leading the way out.

As a follow-up to the story, you might want to pose several related questions to your audience: "What if you were lost in the woods? What would you do?" Then, go over the guidelines in the above section.

**Estimated Telling Time:** 9–10 minutes

# · 20 ·

# Cudjoe's Refuge

Cebe Tate must have felt this way—trapped.

I had waded into a thick wall of titi bushes, pushing my way through, with not even an animal trail to follow. When I stopped to check my compass, I felt branches touching and poking most every part of my body. It was a type of vegetative claustrophobic torture chamber.

At least I wasn't lost like Cebe Tate.

In 1875, Tate wandered into a massive swamp north of Carrabelle to hunt a panther that had been killing his livestock, so the story goes. He got disoriented, snake-bit, and he lost his gun. For seven days he wandered, drinking swamp water and eating whatever he could find. Finally, he crawled out onto a Carrabelle street, his brown hair now white. When someone asked him his name, he rasped, "My name is Cebe Tate, and I just came from hell!"

Tate's Hell. The name stuck.

Today, only a few parts of Tate's Hell resemble what the great swamp was like in the old days. One place is along Tate's Hell's northern boundary—the Mud Swamp/New River Wilderness Area in the Apalachicola National Forest. That's where I began hiking and wading on a bright winter's day. I had a hankering for wild territory, one that few people have ever seen. I wasn't disappointed. This swamp was thousands of acres in size. An unprepared person could get lost.

After pushing through wall after wall of thick bushes and vines, the swamp opened into a muddy expanse of cypress trees and tall grass. This must be the heart of the swamp, I thought, a place for only wild beasts like black bears and wildcats. That's why the human footprint, plain and clear in the mud, surprised me. As I spotted more prints, I quickly determined several things: the person was barefoot, he was likely male, and his left foot was missing a middle toe.

**A hiker makes his way through the Mud Swamp/New River Wilderness Area, part of the broader Tate's Hell Swamp.**

Curiosity rushed through me, but also a chill. Who could he be? And why was he in here?

For the next two hours I followed the footprints as they wound around cypress trees in an erratic pattern. I frequently double-checked my compass. It appeared that the individual was going in no particular direction. In fact, he was making a big circle, most likely lost. He needed help, and I was the only other person for miles around. I intensified my efforts. What had begun as an exploration of a wild place had turned into a mission.

As I neared one of the incredible walls of titi bushes that have made the area nearly impenetrable, I heard a rustling and snapping of twigs ahead. "Hello!" I yelled. "Do you need help?"

At first there was silence. Nothing moved, so I began pushing my way through the bushes, following. That's when I heard the voice, raspy and desperate sounding: "Don't come any closer or I'll stick you!"

I froze. "I'm not going to hurt you," I said in a soft voice. "If you're lost, I can help."

There was silence again. I could barely make out a human form. Perhaps the person was determining if he could trust me. Finally, a voice came forth: "You ain't no slave hunter, are you?"

Jim Lollis pushes his way through thick vegetation in the Mud Swamp/New River Wilderness Area.

"Slave hunter? No, most certainly not. I'm here to help you."

"Are you British?"

"No."

"Spanish."

"No."

"Then you got to be a slave hunter. You ain't taking me back. I'll die first."

*This is really getting weird*, I thought. I was dealing with a deranged person. "I'm from Tallahassee," I shouted.

"You don't sound Muscogee. Tallahassee is a Muscogee town."

Wow, I thought. Who was this person and where was he from? "I'm friends with many Muscogees in Florida," I said, trying to sound convincing. Then, I used the Muscogee term for "How are you?" "*Stong-goh?*"

Silence again. "You got a gun?" he asked.

I wasn't sure how to answer this one. I did not have a gun, but I also wondered if the stranger could be dangerous. "Uh, just a small one," I lied.

When I didn't hear anything else, I decided to give the man some space. "Now, I'm going to back away. If you want me to help you, you come out of there. Otherwise, I'm going home."

I stepped back a few steps. "No, no, wait," the man called to me. "I'm coming out. I've been in this swamp too long."

I stopped and waited for the man to come forward. When I saw him, I tried to keep my jaw from dropping open. He was African American, not quite six feet tall, and his simple clothes appeared to have been torn by a thousand thorns. He bore scars on his wrists and ankles as if he had once worn manacles, and his face had a long scar that traveled around his neck to his back. He clutched a sharpened stick with both hands.

"Er, my name is Doug," I managed to say.

"I'm Cudjoe," he said hesitantly.

"Nice to meet you, Cudjoe. Where you from?"

"Don't pay no never mind to that. I've got to get to the fort. You'll help me, won't you, before the slave hunters find me?"

"Uh, what fort?"

"The Negro Fort on the big river. I've got to get there."

"Okay, let's get out of this swamp first."

I pulled out my compass and set a course for my car. It was parked near a washed-out bridge on an unpaved road. "You hungry or thirsty, Cudjoe? I have trail mix and a bottle of water."

Cudjoe frowned. He looked confused. "No, no thanks. I'm not hungry for that no more."

"How long have you been in here?"

"A long lonesome time," he said. "I been in here a long time."

Sunrays were slanting through treetops when we finally reached my car. After pulling off spiderwebs from my shirt and brushing off my hat, I opened the passenger door for Cudjoe. "Get in, Cudjoe, I'll take you where you need to go."

He stepped back, looking frightened. "What kind of carriage is this? Where's your mules?"

"Hmm, they're inside, built in. Come on."

He sat down nervously. "Is this a chariot of fire, like in the Bible?"

"Kind of like that."

"Are you an angel?"

"No," I said, chuckling. "No one ever asked me that before."

"Then you're the devil?" he shrieked, pulling away.

"Definitely not," I responded firmly, although Betty Mason in third grade once accused me of being a devil for dipping her hair in ketchup at lunchtime.

"Then, what are you?" Cudjoe seemed intent on making sense out of the situation.

"Let's just say I'm here to take you where you need to go," I said.

"Kind of like one of God's messengers?"

"Kind of like that," I replied. It was important not to make Cudjoe agitated or disturbed. He needed help.

"We need to go to the fort then," he said. "I think it's in that direction." He pointed towards the western sun. "I can't go no place else. The fort's where I find my freedom. That place is home."

I nodded. I thought of taking him straight to the police station in Carrabelle but remembered that the station was only a telephone booth. A sign advertised it as the world's smallest police station.

Tallahassee, and possibly Apalachicola, had a psychiatric ward. One look and they'd admit him right away. While I thought about my alternatives, something else stirred inside, beyond rational and logical thinking. Intuitively, my direction became clear: I needed to take Cudjoe to the fort.

As we drove past the tiny town of Sumatra and down more unpaved forest roads, Cudjoe played with the buttons on my radio and with my automatic windows. He hummed to himself, an old chant or hymn I didn't recognize. He looked at me differently now. His countenance of desperation and distrust had been replaced by one of longing and anticipation. He even smiled. When he glanced out the window, he seemed amazed at the speed we were going, like a child on his first train or airplane ride.

"I hope things is the same at the fort," he said. "I hope things haven't changed."

I didn't know what to say, so I kept quiet. I assumed the fort he was talking about was on Prospect Bluff, overlooking the Apalachicola River. The British built it during the War of 1812, and upon their defeat, they turned it over to a group of escaped slaves, free blacks, and Seminole Indians. With the fort, the new owners dreamed of establishing a free country, where people would not be persecuted or forced to work against their wills. Many vowed to fight and die rather than return to the grueling plantations. The fort drew escaped slaves from as far away as Tennessee and Mississippi.

As we neared the river and pulled up to the historic site, Cudjoe's eyes widened. After parking the car, Cudjoe stepped out and rushed past the kiosk that explained how American forces, backed by slave owners seeking escaped slaves, attacked the fort in 1816. During the battle, a warship heated up a cannonball red-hot and shot it toward the fort. It hit the fort's magazine where gunpowder and ammunition were stored. The thunderous explosion killed almost everyone inside and obliterated most of the log walls and buildings, destroying the hopes and dreams of a desperate people.

"There it is!" Cudjoe cried. "It's, it's beautiful." While I saw only grass and trees where the fort once stood, Cudjoe clearly saw something else. Tears rolled down his cheeks. He turned to me. "Thank you.! Thank you!" he said. "I am finally home."

With that he walked forward and vanished. From somewhere, I heard the creaking of large wooden gates opening then closing.


## AUTHOR'S NOTES


Seeds for this story were planted while exploring Mud Swamp, the part of Tate's Hell featured in this story. I had convinced a neighbor to go along with me and enter the big swamp from the east by canoe, following a small creek

**The wild Mud Swamp/New River Wilderness Area.**

called Cat Branch. We hoped to find the New River and a southerly way out. Normally you can't canoe through Mud Swamp because the New River spreads out into a wide silt bottom mud flat covered with downed trees, but the map showed that the river collected itself again somewhere in the swamp and flowed out the southern end. So, if we found this connection, we could be the first to canoe through the swamp.

On a winter's day, the best time for swamp explorations, we worked our way down Cat Branch through a tangle of vines and brush, our boat filling up with spiders. Sweaty and exhausted, we reached the heart of the swamp and, much to our relief, found the New River below the point where we thought it reestablished itself. After some challenging portages over and around cypress knees and logjams, the river suddenly fanned out in several directions through a thick, shadowy forest of cypress and gum trees. Each channel was only a foot or so wide and a couple of inches deep. It was a virtual maze. The canoe could go no farther.

While staring at the incredible jungle of trees and silver ribbons of water, with thin shafts of sunlight barely able to creep through the canopy, I thought how easily Seminole Indians or escaped slaves could have hid undetected. The danger was, of course, that they would become lost in unfamiliar territory. I wondered how many of them did.

In regard to Negro Fort, later named Fort Gadsden, you can visit this historic site by traveling south on Highway 65 from Highway 20. After passing through the tiny town of Sumatra, turn west off Forest Road 129 and follow the signs to the Fort Gadsden historic site.

## MORE ABOUT THE FIRST SEMINOLE WAR

For a brief period in 1815, hope glimmered for a desperate people. The British turned over a fully armed log fort on the Apalachicola River to about three hundred fugitive slaves and a handful of Seminole and Choctaw Indians. As news spread, hundreds of escaped slaves were drawn to the fort and surrounding area. It became known as "Negro Fort."

Following several small skirmishes and mounting pressure from Georgia slaveholders, General Andrew Jackson sent a large naval and ground contingent of American forces and Creek allies to destroy the fort in 1816.

Less than two years later, with hundreds of Seminoles, free blacks, and fugitive slaves reoccupying the Apalachicola River area, General Jackson returned with an even larger force and burned all the villages. Most residents had already fled. Jackson then commissioned Lieutenant James Gadsden to rebuild the old Negro Fort. Gadsden's "talents and indefatigable zeal" prompted the general to name the new structure "Fort Gadsden."

Jackson and his men then swept through North Florida, destroying villages of blacks and Seminoles in Tallahassee, Miccosukee, and along the Suwannee River, engaging in minor skirmishes. He took over the Spanish fort at St. Marks, believing it to be a supply source for the Indians. He found two British traders and hung them. The raids and executions were controversial since Florida was then claimed by Spain, but it did serve to drive the bulk of Seminole Indians and escaped slaves out of North Florida. Also, Spain realized its inability to hold and defend Florida and sold the territory to the United States three years later.

## STORYTELLING TIPS

When speaking for the character Cudjoe, at first keep his tone to one of desperation and distrust. Gradually fill your voice with hope and awe as he nears the fort site. A good follow-up discussion is about the role of escaped slaves in the Seminole wars (also see chapter 14). Pose the question: If you suddenly found yourself in a time period two hundred years in the future, what might you find?

**Estimated Telling Time:** 12–13 minutes

# • *21* •

# Snake Woman

$\mathcal{P}$eople come from all over for the annual Green Corn Ceremony along North Florida's Apalachicola River. Part of the ritual is to stay up late or all night around a special fire to bring in the Muscogee new year. I've attended the gatherings for more than twenty years, and one night stands out, back when I was still single.

I was sitting by the fire well past midnight. We had finished dancing and most participants were resting or feasting at the nearby cook shack. It was rare to find myself alone by the fire, but I was not alone for long. A beautiful woman with long dark hair approached me. She had walked up from the swamp down the hill.

My visitor was thin and wore an old-style Creek Indian dress, the pattern of which looked familiar and made me slightly uncomfortable, but I couldn't figure out why. Beaded earrings spiraled down from her earlobes and bounced slightly when she moved. I assumed this woman was a guest of someone in the camp because I had never seen her before.

"Where are you from?" I asked.

"All over," she replied, gliding into the chair next to me. "It's been a long time. A very long time." She gazed into the fire and smiled then glanced up at me with glowing eyes. "You're from south of Tallahassee, aren't you?"

"Why yes, how did you—"

"Some beautiful forests around there, and springs and sinkholes, and swamps. Those swamps are the wildest places left, aren't they?" I nodded. "Good places to hide," she added.

Something about the woman made me uneasy, but I also appreciated her natural beauty. It was difficult for me to determine her age, especially by firelight. She could have been thirty, forty, or fifty. I wasn't sure, but did I mention her youthful beauty? I found it hard to keep my eyes off her.

143

"Used to be, people would dance here all night," she said, "back in the old days. If some people rested, others would step in. That singing and dancing was something."

"They still do that at some grounds, especially in Oklahoma," I said. "But we're too small here, and we don't have many dance leaders. We stop around midnight."

The woman smiled sadly. "Still, it is peaceful to sit quietly by the fire. Here with you."

Whoaa, I thought. This woman is coming on strong.

"I've been watching you for a long time," she continued.

"You know, I don't believe we've ever met," I responded, trying to stay polite. "My name is Doug."

"I know." She smiled and gazed into the fire, then she glanced up at me, the flames dancing in her dark eyes. "Can I tell you a story?" she asked.

"Sure, I love a good storyteller."

"Good. This is a special story, one that's very old and important to these grounds." I nodded. My curiosity was aroused.

"A long time ago, in the old days," she began, "these grounds were located farther north in the heart of the old Muscogee country, back before Europeans arrived. The Green Corn Ceremony then was very large, and people came from all around. The all-night dance had maybe three or four hundred participants. You should have seen it—a throng of people moving as one around the fire, the male leader shaking a rattle while a hundred or two hundred women danced in rhythm with their ankle shakers. The voices and music carried a long way, to all creatures of the forest. They joined in, too, in their own ways. They appreciated the Muscogee and their dancing.

"For many years, a mysterious woman would visit the grounds during the dances. She wore her hair long in the Muscogee way and the pattern on her leather dress reminded people of something they couldn't quite put their finger on. No one recognized the woman. Everyone assumed she was related to someone else, and so she joined in the dances with no problem.

"At some point during the night, she would choose a dance partner from the village and immediately, the man could not keep his eyes off her, like he was under a spell. Just before dawn, the dance couple would be gone. Nobody remembered seeing them leave, but that wasn't unusual since there were so many people at the ceremony. However, the young man would be missing for several weeks. No one could find a trace of him. When he returned, his legs would be wobbly, and he had no recollection of what had happened to him. The last thing he remembered was dancing with that beautiful woman at the Green Corn Ceremony.

"When the young man would recover, people noticed that his senses were keener. He would be a better hunter and provider. So, whatever happened to him, it somehow benefited him and the people. The village elders were curious and decided to find out more. They instructed two warriors to watch the all-night dances during the coming Green Corn Ceremony and follow the man and woman wherever they went. 'Under no circumstances should you interfere,' they said.

"During the all-night dance of the Green Corn Ceremony, the mysterious woman arrived as always. And just as before, she chose a male partner and danced only with him. Just before dawn, as the two warriors watched closely, the man and woman quietly peeled off from the dance line and left the grounds. The two warriors followed. They could barely keep up. They would climb one hill, only to see the couple on the next hill. This went on for many miles.

"Now, these two warriors were good runners, but they were getting tired. Just as they were about to give up, they saw the couple slow down while climbing a hill. A large live oak tree stood on top, and they watched the couple go behind the tree and not leave. The two warriors approached cautiously. They followed the tracks to the back of the tree where there was a large hollow opening. They looked in and stepped back in surprise. Inside the tree were two large rattlesnakes moving back and forth as if in a mating ritual.

"Since they were instructed not to interfere, the two warriors returned to the village and reported to the elders what they had seen. The elders discussed the matter for several days. They concluded that their mysterious visitor was really a rattlesnake woman who came every year to claim her mate. The pattern on her dress, they now realized, was that of a diamondback rattlesnake. But since the woman obviously did not harm the man she chose, and somehow benefited him and the people, they decided not to interfere. This was powerful medicine. They also realized that a rattlesnake had not struck anyone in the village for several years. Maybe this was because the people were now related."

I interrupted, "Oh, so that must be why some Muscogee people don't kill rattlesnakes—because they might be related."

"That's right," she agreed. "But the story is not finished. An unusual thing happened after the rattlesnake woman was discovered. She did not attend the following Green Corn Ceremony, or several ceremonies after that. Just when the stories told around the fire began to sound like tall tales the children didn't quite believe, that's when she would show up and claim a new mate. She would turn up maybe once or twice every century, and she hasn't showed up at these grounds for a long, long time."

**A coiled diamondback rattlesnake, by Carol Highsmith, Library of Congress.**

The storyteller beamed at me then. I was drawn into the deep pools of her eyes. I felt tingly and helpless. The mysterious woman leaned over and whispered to me, beckoning me with her irresistible beauty. "Dance with me, Doug."

Her hand was cold but powerful. And as we moved around the fire, I felt enfolded by a swirl of light. I heard a hundred rhythmic ankle shakers and a multitude of singing voices, coupled with the loud whir of a rattle.

## AUTHOR'S NOTES

As a young man visiting a Muscogee Creek Indian ceremony for a weekend, I was spellbound one night when an elder relayed the rattlesnake woman story. It stuck with me. And now that I have gray hairs myself, I sometimes share the story with young people who are attending a Muscogee ceremonial

The story I've shared with you is very much like the one I first heard, with some added touches of my own regarding a first-hand encounter with the mythic woman of the Muscogee legend. The story still makes me shiver. Could it somehow be true?

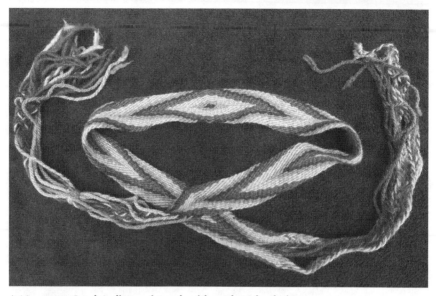

A Muscogee Creek Indian waist sash with rattlesnake design.

## MORE ABOUT THE DIAMONDBACK RATTLESNAKE

Few things will send shivers up your spine than an encounter with an eastern diamondback rattlesnake. The loud vibration of the rattle warns you to keep your distance, and if you continue to approach, the snake will likely coil, hiss, rattle louder, and perhaps strike. Its size alone can prompt one to pause as the diamondback rattlesnake can grow up to eight feet in length with a girth resembling a man's thigh. Tales of giant rattlers exceeding ten feet in length may be just that—tales.

The eastern diamondback is not known to be particularly aggressive, and it doesn't always rattle depending on how well it is camouflaged. Most snakebites occur when people are harassing or handling the snake. It likely developed a rattle to warn large animals such as bison that they were approaching too close, helping to prevent the snake from being trampled. Unfortunately, for the rattlesnake, its rattle often gives away its position to humans wanting to do it harm.

Like most pit vipers, rattlesnakes have heat sensors to help detect prey, such as rodents and rabbits. With this organ, even a blindfolded rattler can locate its prey and deliver an accurate, deadly strike. When striking, the rattler's mouth opens wide and its hollow curved fangs swing out, allowing the snake to stab its victim and inject venom, striking and recoiling in a remarkable one-quarter of a second, or roughly 175 miles per hour. Generally, one strike will suffice.

Although rattlesnakes are not endangered, their numbers have been steadily dropping due to habitat loss, rattlesnake roundups, and the tendency of many people to kill any snake on sight. Few realize that by eating small prey animals, rattlesnakes help keep nature in balance.

Biologist Bruce Means, who has extensively studied the eastern diamond-back rattlesnake, made this conclusion in *BBC Wildlife* magazine:

> Whenever people used to ask me what good rattlesnakes are, I used to give utilitarian answers: their venom is used to make anti-venom for protection against snake-bites, their skin is a valuable leather. After twenty-five years of closely studying the eastern diamondback, I appreciate the species for what it is: a highly evolved life form with very complicated behavior. The gentle-natured eastern diamondback has intrinsic value just as we do. They are "good" simply because they "are."

## STORYTELLING TIPS

An absolute must for telling this story is to shake a hand rattle at the appropriate time, mimicking the vibration of a rattlesnake's rattle.

**Estimated Telling Time:** 9–10 minutes

# · 22 ·

# Muscogee Drum

$\mathcal{A}$ steady beat, as if from a drum, reverberated through the floodplain swamp of the upper Apalachicola River. I knew it wasn't from woodpeckers. They drum on trees in search of insects, but they stop for breaks. This slow, steady beat never stopped—*thump, thump, thump*. Unceasing. It reminded me of something; there was familiarity about it, but I wasn't sure what.

I walked in the direction of the sound. It grew louder, seeming to echo through the trees and across sloughs. Why was someone drumming here, and where were they?

I had come to take photos of the floodplain in fall. Cypress needles had turned a copper gold, sweetgum and swamp maple a brilliant red. Swamp hickories blazed yellow and orange. This was the best place to see fall colors in Florida, but the drumming—or whatever it was—overrode all else. It was as if the river swamp itself was somehow speaking.

I skirted around huge cypress trees. Many were hollow, though still living, with ankle-high knees protruding from the spongy ground. Gnarled tupelo gum trees with expansive cone-shaped bases stood out too. On slightly higher ground, other trees formed a dense canopy. During spring, these forests are normally flooded, but this was fall. Drier weather enabled me to wander freely on foot. A wild place, it had been little disturbed since loggers worked the woods in the 1920s. Normally I would have stopped to take photos, but the steady beat prompted me to keep moving.

Wood smoke. I thought I smelled it. A campfire, perhaps. Then it dissipated as quickly as it came.

*Thump, thump, thump.*

Animals had gone before me. I followed their trails—deer, wild pig, raccoon, opossum, and even a black bear. Occasionally I would glimpse

**Hikers make their way through the wide floodplain of the upper Apalachicola River.**

movement to my left or right, but when I turned, I saw nothing, as if the creatures were playing a game of hide-and-seek. At one point an eagle cried and lifted upward from a pool of water. Once above treetops, it spiraled overhead, seeming to lead me on, its cries mixing with the steady thump in the air.

The drumming softened when I climbed a large rise. Songbirds sang louder than the drum, a chorus of songbirds, more than I had ever heard in one spot. I walked onward, pushing through brush, knocking away spiderwebs. Soon I came upon a clearing that was covered with weeds but little else, as if the earth had been packed too solid for trees to take hold. My feet seemed to penetrate the ground when I walked on it, and a warm feeling rose up through my legs and filled my body and mind. I felt pure, child-like. Then, mixed with the bird calls, I heard human voices singing and smelled the wood smoke even stronger. But no one was around. In a sudden moment of clarity, I understood. This was the place I had heard about, the place my elderly friend Andy told me about years before. He grew up along the river and was proud of his Muscogee Creek Indian heritage.

The Muscogee were once concentrated in Alabama, Georgia, and North Florida. Most were moved west on the Trail of Tears in the 1830s and 1840s, and some fled into the Everglades with the Seminoles. Andy's family was part of a group that hid in the backwoods and swamps of North Florida. He would tell stories of growing up in the area, especially of visiting ceremonial grounds that were hidden among the sloughs and river swamps of the Apalachicola River. Few people knew about them. To be discovered could have brought trouble during a time when being Indian in Florida wasn't popular, or even legal.

Some of the traditional gatherings Andy recalled were of attending the Green Corn Ceremony, a yearly rite of renewal that involved all-night dancing around a special fire and the taking of herbal medicines. A big feast was part of it too. "We'd dig a big pit and roast huge gar fish we caught in the river and sloughs," he said. "Those sure were good."

Most of the dances were called stomp dances. A man would often lead with a hand rattle and women would follow with turtle shells filled with pebbles, called shakers, strapped to their ankles. When the women stomped their feet, the shakers would help keep the rhythm of the dance. Sometimes a man would accompany certain dances by beating on a drum made from a hollow cypress knee, especially for dances performed by the men.

I once asked Andy what happened to the ceremonial grounds. "World War II came along and most of the men moved to Panama City or Pensacola to join the military," he said. "Some never returned, and we never started back up."

My curiosity remained strong. I asked Andy if he would show me the old grounds. "It's best to just leave things be," he said, and sighed. There were newer ceremonial grounds that Muscogee people visited, and Andy was active at one of them on the edge of a county park. Being Indian was more acceptable these days, he said, but the ceremonies were shorter—squeezed into a weekend—because people led busier lives. "At the old grounds, the ceremonies would go on for days," he said. "And we'd be deep in those river swamps where no one would find us, feeling a part of everything as if nothing had changed in thousands of years. It was a place we could be Indian again, a place to feel free."

I slowly circled the old grounds, wondering what it was like—all-night dances, feasts of wild food, storytelling, lively Muscogee games. This was the focal point of a people who carried on their ancient ways, and now, it was no more. I listened. The drumming was still present, but faint. *Thump, thump, thump.*

I wanted to stay, but the sun was dipping lower in the west. When I stepped off the rise and back down into the floodplain, the drumming became loud again, seeming to come from every direction. I remembered Andy saying the Muscogee rarely used drums, unlike native people of the western Plains.

Muscogee drums were small and for specific dances, he said. So why did I keep hearing a drumbeat? Suddenly, I knew. I recognized the sound. The rhythm was not from a drum but from a slow and steady heartbeat, one that never stopped, the heartbeat of a nearly forgotten people. And it lived on in the wild Apalachicola River swamps.

## AUTHOR'S NOTES

A confederation of several tribes, the Muscogee Creek Indians once lived throughout the southeastern United States. They built complex ceremonial centers and large towns with expansive farms, mostly along rivers. After the first Europeans arrived in the early 1500s, disease took a great toll on the population. Eventually European and then American settlers took more and more Muscogee land. Finally, when Andrew Jackson became president in 1829, he pushed the Indian Removal Act through Congress, forcing the removal of more than twenty thousand Muscogee Creek Indians. This came to be known as the Trail of Tears. They were resettled in what is now Oklahoma.

Small Muscogee Creek Indian groups remained in Florida and other parts of their homeland by intermarrying with either white or black families, hiding their Indian identity. Some carried on their customs and ceremonial ways in secret for several generations, the subject of this story.

## STORYTELLING TIPS

Ideally, this story should be told with a drum. You can beat the drum softly or loudly, depending on what part of the story you are telling.

**Estimated Telling Time:** 8–9 minutes

# • 23 •

# Ghost Gator

$C$ooter had never spent much time with his son Matt. He and his ex-wife, Marilyn, split up nine years before when she moved Matt and his two sisters three hundred miles to Jacksonville. Their townhouse was about as different as one could get from Cooter's cabin along the Choctawhatchee River. Not surprisingly, and a relief for Matt's mother, Cooter rarely visited their new home. She often said that when Cooter bled, his blood wasn't red but the color of swamp water. Cities were about the only thing to strike fear in the self-described swamp rat. That's why Matt was shocked when Cooter showed up during the last week of summer break and insisted on taking him alligator hunting.

Marilyn didn't like it. "You can't take that boy. He's got too much city in him now."

"That's why I had to come, before it's too late."

"Too late for what?"

"To teach him the ways of the swamp. To take him on his first gator hunt. Got me a permit this time."

Marilyn rolled her eyes and shook her head. "I'll leave it up to him then. He's old enough now. How about it, Matt?" She turned to her gangly fourteen-year-old.

Matt wasn't sure. He enjoyed basketball and video games and going out with his friends. Gator hunting? What did alligators ever do to him?

"Come on, son," Cooter insisted. "It's time you learned to be a man."

Matt looked into his father's pleading eyes, a man he barely knew. He didn't want to make it harder for his mother. He remembered the fights they

153

used to have. Cooter spent too much time in the swamp, she'd say, and come home smelling of fish, reptiles, sweat, and beer. She yearned for finer things, city things, and so she left him and took the kids. She didn't tell Cooter where she was heading—she didn't know for sure—but Cooter tried to track them down as he did a wild animal. When he finally found them weeks later, he'd had a crazed look, like he was going to skin them all and stretch out their skins to dry. But Marilyn didn't back down. She gave Cooter a choice—live in the swamp or live with them in the city. Cooter chose the swamp, but he didn't feel complete without passing down his swamp ways to his first-born.

"What'll it be, son?" asked Cooter, shifting uncomfortably.

"Okay, I'll go," said Matt.

Marilyn exhaled loudly. She had been holding her breath. "You have him back by the time school starts," she warned Cooter. Her tone meant business.

"That don't give me much time," said Cooter, "but it's a start. Come on, Matt. Get some extra clothes and come on. This city's seeping into my pores like poison."

The next afternoon, Matt found himself gliding through the Choctawhatchee's dark waters, the bright sun hurting his eyes. School would not come soon enough as far as he was concerned. Not only was the hardwooden seat on Cooter's sixteen-foot "Gator King" johnboat uncomfortable, the wooden floor had developed a slow leak beside his left foot. Matt didn't care if the boat had been passed down for three generations. His father needed a new one.

Cooter spit a stream of tobacco into the water and spoke over the drone of the motor. "Yeah, son, your granddaddy skinned gators and his daddy skinned gators, and now you and I are going to skin gators. It's an honest living." Cooter spat into the water again, his nostrils widening. "Only a couple of gators ever got away from my sights once I beaded on them, and one of them's the ghost gator. There aren't many second chances out here and the sooner you learn that the better off you'll be. Gator hunting will teach you about life."

"Ghost gator?" Matt asked, surprised. "The one that's all white?" He remembered childhood tales of the mysterious monster gator.

"Same one. He's still around—big like the gators of old. Thirteen, maybe fourteen-foot-long, and white as a sheep. They say the ghost gator is the gators' way of getting back at us men."

Matt shivered like he always did when he heard stories about the ghost gator.

"You believe all them stories?" Cooter asked, laughing. "Those was just bedtime stories for you kids, about it being a ghost and all. I bet the ghost

**Large alligator sunning along the Wakulla River.**

gator is just an albino. That can happen, you know, a white albino gator, just like with other critters. Thought I shot it once, but I never saw him again. That skin would have fetched a pretty penny."

Matt wanted to change the subject. Ghost or not, he had no desire to meet up with the white gator, especially at night. "Ma said something about there not being many gators left, because of hunting and all?"

"For awhile there wasn't many, so we cut back on the hunting, but they've come back—big time. There will always be gators 'cause Mother Nature wouldn't have it no other way. They're survivors. The only thing that threatens gators are them fools who drain the swamps for farms and condos. These swamps are important for all kinds of life, including fish and oysters down by the Gulf."

Cooter turned into a narrow slough and cut the motor. "Get that paddle there and let's get deeper into the swamp. Daylight's burning." Cooter plunged a worn paddle into the dark water, pulling with hairy, sinewy arms. He plunged the paddle in again, driving it like an angry piston. The swamp absorbed his strokes. Matt marveled at his father's strength, but he couldn't fathom spending days and nights killing gators, sleeping in a boat, and eating canned meats. After a nine-year break from Cooter, he was a green teenager with braces who dreamed of building bridges like his new stepfather. Alligator

**A shadowy river slough in evening.**

hunting wasn't even listed in the career booklet his guidance counselor had given him.

Cooter pointed to a wild boar rooting along the shore. Its tusks and fur separated him from his tame cousins. The boar grunted loudly upon seeing them and crashed through the palmettos. Cooter grinned. "Ain't no place wilder than this here river swamp," he said, eyes gleaming. "No place."

Matt's eyes wandered over the banks, searching for the boar. An image of his mother came to him, the time she wore a beautiful yellow dress at Easter— a dress that matched her long flowing hair.

Cooter smashed a horsefly on a sweat-soaked arm. After checking trot lines for fish, Cooter sat back and sighed. "All this work can make a man tired and thirsty." He wiped his hands on his overalls and popped open a beer. He tossed Matt a soda.

They tied up under a tree and passed sardines, Vienna sausages, and crackers back and forth. Matt relaxed a bit, glancing shyly at his father's un-shaven face. His father could be tough and demanding, but Matt remembered Cooter's soft side too, like the time he brought home baby squirrels that had been blown from their nest. They hand-raised them to adulthood and let them go. "Never kill what you don't need," Cooter told them, "and never waste what you do."

Cooter leaned back and smiled. "Now this is alright, just you and me sitting here after all these years," he exclaimed, slurping his beer. "I know schooling is important—heard you was doing real good, but this place is a type of school too. Snakes, fish, turtles, bugs, birds, gators—they're all important, and they all got something to teach. Even the leaves on the trees—they keep the swamp cool, and after they fall, they turn into food for something else." Matt noticed an egret poking along the shore, bright white against the swamp's deep shadows and dark water. "Killed my first big gator out here about the time I was your age," Cooter continued. "Never been the same since."

The afternoon heat was growing. Both father and son yawned. "Why don't we get some shuteye," said Cooter. "There's plenty to do tonight. Maybe you'll get your first gator." They spread oily bug repellent on their face and hands before leaning back against the boat gunnels. Cooter was soon snoring while Matt slept fitfully on the wet boat bottom, a handful of screaming mosquitoes and horseflies keeping him company. When he dreamed, it was of the white alligator—the ghost gator—and it was coming toward him.

Cooter was the first to awaken. He glanced around. Bats were whisking in and out of the canopy. A barred owl hooted, and another answered. And from deep in the growing shadows he heard an alligator bellow. The swamp man nudged Matt in the foot. "Time to get up, son. Gators are coming alive!"

As Matt rose, he noticed how the swamp had changed. Cypress tops were tinted orange from the setting sun. Still water captured the colorful image. Cooter interpreted his dazed look as one of wonder. "Ain't nothing better than this, son, nothing better."

Paddling the faded green "Gator King," Cooter seemed to know every bend and snag. He said he had a special place in mind, one that once thrived with alligators. "Maybe it'll be like the old days," he said, "and you'll see the glory of hunting the swamp king."

Shadows pressed in. Half-submerged willows, their bark dark and scaly, seemed to grope at them with octopus-like arms. Spanish moss hung from tree branches like clumps of gray flesh.

Cooter's eyes widened. His hands twitched as if he could feel the presence of large reptiles. "You want to kill the first one?" he whispered. "Remember, we have to get right up on them."

"Uh, you go ahead and show me how it's done," Matt stammered.

They switched positions in the boat and Cooter wordlessly gave Matt the flashlight while he put on a headlamp. They floated past a thick clump of trees. Cooter fumbled for his metal spear, one attached to a cable. He had rehearsed this moment with Matt earlier—spear the gator, pull him in, shoot him in the back of the head with a shotgun, tie his mouth shut, and haul him into the boat. "Now," he whispered. Matt flicked on the light and scanned the shore. Two bright red alligator eyes soon appeared. Then they spotted two more and two more after that. "What luck," Cooter exclaimed, "just like the old days. Hold it right there."

They drifted toward two eyes that were the widest distance apart. "It must be a big bull gator," said Cooter excitedly, "a real swamp king. Let's drift a little closer." Cooter flicked on his headlamp and raised the spear.

The boat hit a cypress knee and rocked suddenly. A deep roar emerged from the shadows as an ominous white tail thrashed in the water. The ghost gator! Matt shuddered. Cooter leaned over. "That's the one I've been after!" he cried.

As the boat swung around backward, a willow branch hit Cooter squarely in the back. It happened so quickly that Cooter's mouth simply hung open. He didn't have time to speak. He jolted forward, the spear popping from his hands. He hit the gunnel and rolled into the dark water. The boat pitched and threw Matt to the floor. He scrambled for the shotgun and picked it up, moving to a kneeling position. He pumped, aimed, and fired at the ominous white form advancing toward where Cooter had fallen. The water seemed to explode. Matt pumped and fired again. The water was alive with thrashing and splashing sounds. "Pa! Are you alright?" Matt screamed.

A large white alligator at Gatorland, by Doug Alderson. White alligators can either be albino or have a loss of pigmentation known as leucism.

The white gator emerged from the dark depths, opened his menacing jaws, and let out a blood-curling roar. Then he sunk deep, out of sight. Matt's arms shook and his ears rang from the shots. "Pa!" he cried again, but his voice seemed to be swallowed by a rising chorus of tree frogs and cicadas. Matt frantically scanned the water with the flashlight. Nothing. He was surprised at the sense of loss he felt, as if some part of the swamp—and himself—had died and would never be replaced.

Matt jumped when a wet hand grabbed the side of the boat and Cooter arose, sputtering. "That's a ghost gator alright. You can't kill it, but it can't kill you either."

Matt fainted then, for the first time in memory. When he awoke it was morning and he was at the swamp cabin. Cooter set a bowl of squirrel stew before him. "We'll put off gator hunting for another day," he announced, smiling. "Soon as you finish your breakfast, I'll show you how to catch monster catfish with your bare hands."

## AUTHOR'S NOTES

I've met people like Cooter, the father character in this story. They sometimes refer to themselves as swamp rats or river rats. They normally grew up along a swamp or river and came to know it better than anyone. Their families were generally poor and depended on the fish, wildlife, and alligators in order to survive. Sometimes they supplemented their income by selling illegal moonshine and poaching alligators for their valuable hides.

Florida's colorful swamp rats and river rats are rapidly fading as the state becomes urbanized and conservation laws are better enforced. You can learn more by reading the autobiography of the late Totch Brownm, *Totch: A Life in the Everglades*, swamp rat of the famed Everglades/Ten Thousand Islands region.

## MORE ABOUT ALLIGATORS

Once in danger of becoming extinct, alligator numbers have rebounded to where about two million alligators live in Florida's swamps, lakes, and rivers. Today, limited hunting is allowed and commercial markets for alligator products are tightly regulated.

Alligators are unique reptiles in many ways. Unlike snakes and turtles, a mother alligator will protect her nest and her young for up to two years, fending off predators such as birds, raccoons, bobcats, otters, snakes, and other alligators. The babies often ride on her back. These protective instincts may give us clues about early dinosaurs.

Alligator nests are built above the high-water line. The female alligator creates a mound of leaves, branches, limbs, grasses, and other vegetation that can be more than three feet high and seven feet across, resembling a small haystack. After mating in the spring, females lay between twenty to fifty eggs in early summer. Baby alligators usually hatch in late summer after incubating for two months. The hatchlings are six to eight inches long.

A baby alligator grows about a foot a year for the first five years. Males can grow up to fifteen feet when fully mature, although ten to twelve feet is more common. Females rarely exceed nine feet in length. They can live more than fifty years in the wild and sometimes longer in captivity.

Throughout their lives, alligators play a vital role in the wetland's ecology, especially in the Everglades, by creating ponds that often retain water during drought periods. Many species of birds, mammals, insects, fish, and other aquatic life depend on these ponds for survival. Without the alligator, long feared and hunted by man, the quality of our wetlands would be drastically reduced. Alligators also help to protect wading bird rookeries by eating raccoons and opossums that prey upon the nests, even though alligators may occasionally eat some of the birds they protect.

As Florida's human population expands and encroaches upon alligator habitat, conflicts will likely continue to rise. The state receives thousands of complaints about nuisance alligators each year. Occasionally, alligators become aggressive, especially those that have been fed by people and have lost their natural fear of humans.

## STORYTELLING TIPS

When the ghost gator roars, spread your arms apart and slap them together as you mimic the roar, giving your audience a good jolt.

A great follow-up to this story would be a presentation by a licensed alligator trapper or a trained animal handler who can show your audience a live baby alligator. You may want to visit most any Florida waterway or swamp on a warm night and shine a strong flashlight to find red glowing alligator eyes.

**Estimated Telling Time:** 15–17 minutes

# • 24 •

# The Haunted Book

•

$\mathcal{T}$he townspeople called her a witch. She had lived alone in the swamp for as long as anyone could remember. People reported seeing strange lights and hearing animal sounds coming from her cabin, and on several occasions she was spotted pulling dead animals off the swamp highway and carrying them away. One month, when she didn't come into town for supplies, a brave man checked on her and found her dead. He buried her behind the cabin, said a quick prayer, and hurried home before dark. That was that, except it wasn't. People reported seeing the same eerie lights and hearing the same type of animal and bird calls coming from the house.

Cheyenne had heard the stories for months, ever since the old woman passed away. At ten years old she was curious about a lot of things and often drove adults crazy with endless questions. When no one could give her satisfactory answers about the swamp cabin, she decided to find out for herself.

One Saturday morning Cheyenne loaded a daypack with snacks, water, and bug repellent, and set out toward the cabin. Cobwebs and branches covered the old dirt trail, and whining mosquitoes didn't help. She picked her way through the fern-covered bottomlands, pushing aside vines and Spanish moss, and leaping over small creeks. She often glimpsed movement out of the corner of her eye—flashes of animals or birds—but when she looked directly in that direction, nothing was ever there.

Cheyenne was relieved when she spotted the cabin's gray cypress boards and tilting front porch. Taking a deep breath, she climbed the creaking front steps. The old oak door was closed, but when she reached for the tarnished knob, the door flung open and cold air rushed past. Cheyenne shivered. "Hello!" she called. Hearing no response, she crept forward into a shadowy room. It smelled faintly of wood smoke and rat poop. Cockroaches scurried

**Deer along the Wakulla River.**

about. She felt cold. Once past the door, it slammed shut behind her. Cheyenne jumped, turned around, and grabbed for the knob. It didn't turn. She
was locked in. She thought about climbing out one of the windows, smashing
one if she had to, but a sense of curiosity took over. She reminded herself of
why she came, and she reminded herself to breathe.

Cheyenne slowly moved through the dim room. A kitchen was off to
one side and a bedroom to another, but what drew her attention was the
mantel. A dusty book lay sideways atop it, and from its pages, a faint green
glow shone against the wall. She carefully took the book into her hands. As
if by magic, the front door flung open and a cold wind pushed her toward it.
She didn't resist. Clutching the book, she bolted from the cabin, descended
the steps, and sped down the trail. It seemed that many life-forms were moving with her—animals and birds, even insects—however she saw nothing
but flashes of feather and fur, and wings. It was only when she reached her
bedroom that Cheyenne examined the book's worn leather cover. The title
was barely readable. Some letters had worn away: *Th Gi l   ith  he Mag c W
nd.* "The Girl with the Magic Wand," she read aloud. Cheyenne opened the
book and began reading the yellowed pages.

The girl in the story seemed familiar to Cheyenne. She spoke, behaved,
and even had long brown hair just like she did. In fact, her name was Cheyenne! The story was about her searching for a magic wand in the attic of an

**1880s cabin at the Tallahassee Museum like the one featured in the story.**

abandoned house. Once she found the wand, she began to do magic things, even bringing dead animals and pets back to life. A spell was given for the feat: "You whose life has been taken are now whole again. Live as you were, not as you are, and come forth." In real life, Cheyenne loved animals and often felt heartbroken when they were killed or injured.

Cheyenne read on and on. She hardly ate any of her dinner before rushing back to the book, and when Monday came, she brought the book to school and couldn't resist pulling it out of her daypack and reading it during math class, trying to shield the pages with a sheet of arithmetic problems. Mr. Killebrew was surprised to spot her deception. Cheyenne had always been a good student. "What is so special about that book?" he asked. Cheyenne tried to explain but Mr. Killebrew gently took the book from her hands. "I'll just have to find out for myself."

After fifteen minutes the class found Mr. Killebrew reading the book at his desk. He didn't look up. All they could see was his almost-bald head tilted over the open book. Oh no, Cheyenne thought, the book has him under some sort of spell.

Mr. Killebrew didn't stop reading, even after Johnny Stewart threw a paper wad at Katherine Monks and she threw one back. Most of the class was soon having a huge paper wad fight—right in front of the teacher! Finally,

Cheyenne stood up and walked toward Mr. Killebrew, dodging flying paper wads. "Mr. Killebrew. Mr. Killebrew!" she called. He didn't answer. When Cheyenne reached over the desk and yanked the book from his hands, he looked up. "Oh, hello, Cheyenne. Is class over already? My, that is an enchanting book. No wonder you love it so much. And it's so strange that the lead character is a boy named Tums. Why, that used to be my nickname! I once had a rather large tummy."

"I thought it was a girl named Cheyenne," she protested.

"Oh no, most definitely Tums, and it describes me when I was a boy perfectly."

Cheyenne frowned as she tucked the book into her daypack.

During dinner, Cheyenne had trouble eating. She moved the carrots into the peas, and the peas and carrots into the potatoes, and then she tried to separate them all out again.

"Cheyenne, what is the matter with you?" her mother asked. "Is everything all right at school?"

"Oh Mom, it's that book I've been reading. Mr. Killebrew started reading it at school and got caught in some kind of spell. Kids started throwing paper wads and going crazy."

Cheyenne's mother couldn't stop laughing. "You mean that book is haunted or something?" She howled louder.

"Mom, see for yourself. You start—" Cheyenne stopped herself, but it was too late. Her mother pulled the book from her daypack.

Cheyenne woke up the next morning not knowing what to expect. The sun shone bright through her window. The sun! Her mother usually woke her before sunrise on school days.

"Mom! Mom!" Cheyenne screamed. She ran to her mother's bedroom. She was sitting up in bed reading THE BOOK! "Mom, you're late for work and I'm late for school!"

Her mother reluctantly put down the book. "Really? Why, I just started reading this wonderful story a little while ago—around eleven o'clock, I think."

"Eleven o'clock at night?"

"Of course, silly."

"You mean you haven't slept all night?"

Her mother glanced out the window with a shocked expression on her face. "I, I guess not."

Before Cheyenne hurried to school that day, she put the book in the big black trash barrel beside the curb in front of her house. Garbage pickup would be that afternoon. Then, the troublesome book would be gone forever!

That night, somewhere during her dream about Mr. Killebrew requiring the whole class to read the haunted book for an English assignment, Cheyenne

Old book like the haunted book in the story.

heard a loud thumping sound at her front door. At first she thought a tree branch was banging against it, or maybe some lost night bird. Finally, curiosity took hold and she flicked on her light, walked to the front door, and peeked out through the peephole. No one was there. She creaked open the door and a heavy object fell beside her foot. The book! It had found its way back, and it didn't smell too good.

Cheyenne knew what she had to do. The next morning she faked a stomach virus and stayed home from school. Once her mother left for work, she tucked the book under her arm and set out toward the old cabin. Once again, she felt many creatures moving down the trail with her, but she never saw them. At the cabin, the front door lay wide open. She entered and promptly returned the book to the mantel. This was only step one. She pulled a flashlight from her daypack and walked to the kitchen finding two-by-fours nailed against a wall creating a ladder that led to a loft. She boldly climbed to the top. Against the back wall a violet light streamed out from what looked to be a crack in a long box. She flicked on her flashlight and spotted a cedar chest. With trembling hands, she opened the chest and found the item for which she searched—a slender, smooth stick, dark with age. A week before, she would have thought it to be a chopstick of some sort, but not now. This stick had a very specific purpose.

She climbed down from the loft and walked out the back door. She soon found a mound of dirt about six feet long and three feet wide. She pointed the stick toward it and spoke forcefully: "You whose life has been taken are now whole again. Live as you were, not as you are, and come forth!"

Purple light shot out of the stick illuminating the ground and shaking everything around it. Cheyenne was knocked flat on her back. When she looked up, an elderly woman in a flowing blue dress stood before her. Her gray hair billowed out as if caught in an updraft. "Stand up, brave child," she said. "I am Eloise." Cheyenne scrambled to her feet, amazed at how the woman hovered a few inches above the ground. Eloise continued, "Because of you, I can now rest in peace. My natural life is over, but you can carry on the work of helping the animals."

"What animals?" Cheyenne asked.

"The ones carelessly shot and wounded, the ones run over because people drive too fast, the ones abandoned to the elements. I was the keeper of this swamp, and now the wand has been passed to you. You are a friend to the animals. They have chosen you."

Cheyenne saw them then, spirits of deer, bobcat, otter, bear, alligator, snake, woodpecker, hawk, owl, and many others, facing her in a half circle. "Only love can keep them alive," said Eloise, "and a little help from their friends."

"But how can I—"

"You will know," Eloise asserted. "The wand will guide you, and so will the animals. Now, I must go."

With that, Eloise lifted higher, past the treetops, seemingly carried by a great number of butterflies and birds. Then her spirit streaked upward through the sky like a shooting star. Calls from every bird and beast filled the air, rising then falling when the light vanished.

The wand glowed in Cheyenne's hand as if infused with Eloise's spirit. Turning to leave, she knew she was not alone. The animals were with her, and she had work to do.

## AUTHOR'S NOTES

I first made up a similar version of this story for my daughter when she was young. I inserted her name as the lead character to help stimulate her interest. It worked. I always embarrassed her a bit if I told the story to other kids, but she liked it. So, I've kept her name in the story.

"The Haunted Book" is meant to convey many things. First, soon after learning to read, I discovered that books could be magical. Skillfully crafted

**Baby raccoon in tree.**

words and pictures were captivating, sending me to distant lands and periods of time, past or future, even to fantasy worlds. How many of us have picked up a book and found it difficult to put down? The idea of a "haunted" book is not that far-fetched.

Another point I wanted to convey is the impact roads and vehicles have on our wildlife, and the dedication of people who try to rehabilitate injured wildlife. Wouldn't it be wonderful if we could wave a magic wand and restore sick and injured creatures? Unfortunately, it isn't that easy. Rehabilitation of an injured animal or bird can take days, weeks, and even years, and some never recover. Dedicated wildlife rehabilitators need our full support.

## MORE ABOUT HELPING INJURED AND ORPHANED ANIMALS

Many measures can be taken to help injured and orphaned animals, but you must first determine if an animal needs assistance. Simply finding a young animal alone doesn't mean it's abandoned. Many wildlife parents leave their young alone while they are searching for food. This can be true of young birds, rabbits, squirrels, raccoons, fawns, and other types of animals.

Young birds learning to fly, for example, are often hopping on the ground for a few days, and if you watch from a distance, you'll often spot parents feeding it. Leave these birds alone. If the young bird is not feathered, however, or has mostly downy feathers, it has likely fallen from its nest and needs to be put back. First warm the bird in your hands if it's cold. Since most birds do not have a sense of smell, it is a myth that once you touch a baby bird the parents will not accept it. If you can't locate or reach the nest, create a new one from a margarine container or plastic berry basket. Cut drainage holes, add straw or grass, wire it to a nearby bush or tree, and gently place the baby bird inside. Watch from a distance to see if the parent birds come to the peeping baby.

Birds of prey on the ground sometimes appear to be injured when they are hunched over their prey with wings outstretched, but this is simply a protective gesture to deter competitors.

According to the Humane Society of the United States, here's some signs to look for to determine if an animal needs assistance:

- A wild animal brought by a cat or dog
- Bleeding
- An apparent or obvious broken limb or wing
- A featherless or nearly featherless bird (nestling) on the ground
- Shivering
- Evidence of a dead parent nearby

If a wild animal exhibits any of these signs, several organizations in your area might provide assistance. These may include a licensed wildlife rehabilitator, animal shelter, animal control agency, wildlife/exotic animal veterinarian, nature center, wild bird store, or a state wildlife agency. If you feel you can't wait for a wildlife professional and want to capture a wounded animal yourself, think of your own safety first. Injured animals may bite, scratch, or poke, not realizing you are trying to help. A towel, blanket, coat, or gloves can help protect your arms and hands. And always scrub exposed skin after handling any wild animal. Be especially careful around busy roads and highways, as vehicles have injured and killed well-meaning rescuers.

Unless you are trained, don't try to care for the animal yourself. Different animals have different dietary and medical requirements. It is also illegal to keep certain wild animals without proper permits. Place the injured animal in a secure container such as a ventilated cardboard box or cat or dog carrier, keeping it warm but not hot, and take it to a licensed wildlife rehabilitator or veterinarian for care. Birds will often become calm when you restrict their vision, so keep the container dark. Do not give the animal food or water immediately as they are often in shock and eating or drinking can worsen their condition. While in the car, keep the animal out of direct sun, heat, or air conditioning, and maintain a quiet environment.

By educating ourselves and following basic guidelines, we can be of assistance to wild creatures.

## STORYTELLING TIPS

A good prop for this story is a worn antique book. While telling the story, you may want to let your voice drift off and start quietly reading the book, making your audience wonder if you really are under a spell. By establishing a plant in the audience beforehand, they can come up at this point and pry the book from your hands, breaking the mysterious hold it has on you.

This story could complement a visit by or a visit to a licensed wildlife rehabilitator. To see an owl with a broken wing or a gopher tortoise with a cracked shell can drive home the reality of our impact on wildlife. Also, licensed wildlife rehabilitators often welcome volunteer help, even for a short while. So, even if it is cleaning cages, the help is appreciated.

**Estimated Telling Time:** 12–13 minutes

# About the Author

In writing tales for this book, **Doug Alderson** drew upon many years of entertaining young people as a summer camp counselor and storyteller, and also from decades as a swamp explorer.

His love for the outdoors and cultural history prompted a writing career that has spanned decades. He is the author of several books, including *Wild Florida Waters, The Great Florida Seminole Trail, Waters Less Traveled, New Dawn for the Kissimmee River, Encounters with Florida's Endangered Wildlife,* and *A New Guide to Old Florida Attractions*, which the Florida Writers Association placed in the top five of published books for 2017. He has won four first place Royal Palm Literary awards for travel books and several other state and national writing and photography awards. Additionally, his articles and photographs have been featured in magazines such as *Sea Kayaker, Coast and Kayak, Wildlife Conservation, Native Peoples, American Forests, Sierra, Mother Earth News,* and *A.T. Journeys*.

He is also an adventurer, having hiked the entire Appalachian Trail, coordinated a group walk across the United States, backpacked through Europe, and mapped a 1,500-mile sea kayaking trail around Florida. He received the inaugural Environmental Service Award by Paddle Florida in 2015 "for conspicuous commitment, unflagging dedication and love of Florida's natural environment."

For more information, log onto www.dougalderson.net.